The Coffee Shoppe Killer

Inspired by a Shocking True Crime Story

Rod Kackley

Published by Rod Kackley, 2017.

THE COFFEE SHOPPE KILLER

First edition. June 27, 2017.

Written by Rod Kackley.

"I know what I did was horrendous and wrong. I felt so miserable like I couldn't go on. I would have ended it all but I didn't have the courage to kill myself."

— Mary Eileen Sullivan

One

Mary Eileen Sullivan was closing up the Coffee Shoppe, getting ready to head home, thinking about the slob who was waiting for her at the dining room table. That was only partially true. The slob was not really waiting for her. Actually he could not have cared less about her. The slob was so wrapped up in his own pathetic little life that he wouldn't even hear Mary Eileen when she walked through the front door of her — not his — apartment.

As she was locking the front door, Mary Eileen thought back to the morning, more than seventeen hours ago, when she was opening the door of the boutique coffee and bakery. Again, she was thinking about her life and how she wanted it to change when her purse got caught between her hip and the door.

The Beretta .22-caliber pistol inside the bag poked her in the side. Mary Eileen couldn't help smiling.

Christina, one of her employees, had been opening the Coffee Shoppe with Mary Eileen. She bumped into her boss and looked at Mary Eileen with a raised eyebrow as if to ask what was wrong.

"Oh nothing," said Mary Eileen, who didn't need to hear the words to understand Christina's question,"absolutely nothing."

Indeed, nothing was wrong.

Mary Eileen's plan was finally coming together.

She had a good life. But it wasn't perfect, yet. However, the thirty-four-year-old woman with shoulder-length auburn hair and an hourglass figure had been feeling better the past week. She had a new lover.

He wasn't perfect. But Mary Eileen thought he was certainly better than her ex-husband, David Van Holt.

"What a loser," Mary Eileen muttered to herself as she angrily rattled the front door to make sure the Coffee Shoppe was locked tight before she went upstairs to her two-bedroom apartment.

Her life wasn't perfect yet. Actually, it pretty much sucked. But now Mary Eileen had created a plan. And, like the business coaches said, she was ready to work the plan. And Mary Eileen was confident that once she worked her plan better days would be ahead.

The plan?

First, David had to go.

David was worse than a loser, as far as Mary Eileen was concerned.

He was a lazy, ugly, scheming bully.

"You stupid bitch," he yelled more than once. David was berating her this time for burning a dinner. "And you can't even apologize correctly."

Mary Eileen had tried to stammer out a request for forgiveness. But her Irish accent got in the way, just like it always did. Others thought it was beautiful. David did not.

"You live in America now, stupid. You need to learn to speak American," David had demanded more than once. "You sound like a shanty Irish chambermaid off an old PBS TV show."

It is true, Mary admitted to herself. I really should learn to speak like the Americans.

She had come to the United States alone, tired of the strife of her hometown, a village of bombed out buildings in Northern Ireland. Mary Eileen was Catholic to the core, through and through. She loved Ireland. She loved the people and of course, she loved her family.

But Mary Eileen had hated the violence.

As a child, in the 1970s, she would walk to school being looked down upon by British soldiers who patrolled the village with giant German Shepherd dogs. At least they looked like giants, or at the very least, horses to Mary Eileen and her third-grade classmates.

She dreamed of an escape every day until she was sixteen years of age and could flee on her own.

Mary Eileen had signed up as a foreign exchange student her last year of school. The air flight was free. Once she landed at LaGuardia in New York all she had to do was to run, and run she did.

Making her life in New York as an attractive, blue-eyed, freckle-faced teenager was easy. There was always an old man — middle-aged really — but old to Mary Eileen, who was willing to pay her money for a favor.

She had saved her money for more than sixteen years as she traveled west before landing in St. Isidore, Michigan. There were plenty of Catholics. It was a small, slow town; at least compared to New York. And the people who lived there, Mary Eileen found, were very charitable.

In fact, they were more than charitable and they didn't ask for anything in return.

Mary Eileen had found a home.

She was able to find an apartment through a group called Liz's House by inventing just a slight lie about being abused by her boyfriend; a boyfriend that she never had. But she knew how to spin a tale and this one worked well enough for room and board.

Mary Eileen finished high school through a GED program, got her diploma and then went on to St. Isidore Community College where she learned the basics of running her own business.

But she never lost her brogue, her Irish accent. If anything, Mary Eileen refined her accent. It worked wonderfully with the first people she met who fell in love with her and her stories of Ireland.

She spun her Irish heritage into the Coffee Shoppe, using it to her advantage, to make her business different from the dozens of other coffee shops that lined South DeVos Avenue in St. Isidore's Heartside District.

Mary Eileen was on the poor end of town. But that was okay. The downtown office workers who spent their days on the other side of Fulton Street seemed more than happy to spend their money with her.

They would listen to her stories about Ireland, eating her baked goods, drinking her coffee, and not working on their laptops. They even seem to get a little bit of a thrill stepping over the homeless bums who seemed to always be sleeping on the Coffee Shoppe's doorstep.

"Gives the place atmosphere," Christina had said to Mary Eileen a few mornings before as they tried to push one of the sleepers off the steps with their feet.

Mary Eileen had punctuated her disgust with the absurdity of that optimism by giving the bum a swift kick in the back, hoping she got his kidneys.

Mary Eileen knew her own mind. That's why no one worked on their laptops in the Coffee Shoppe. As far as Mary Eileen was concerned, coffee shops were for talking, making friends, or even staring out the window thinking about life. She had very few rules. But one thing Mary Eileen insisted on was that nobody in the Coffee Shoppe would spend their time with their bodies bent like question marks pecking away on their laptops or smartphones.

That worked too. It made the Coffee Shoppe different.

And Mary Eileen was different. That worked for everyone but David.

All of her customers spoke American. The maintenance people who were constantly working on the pipes in the cellar of the ice cream shop spoke American. There were some accents, but none as thick as hers. There didn't seem to be anyone in St. Isidore who didn't speak the language of America.

So, David was right about the language.

But, David was wrong about Mary Eileen being stupid, and he knew it.

Mary Eileen just sounded like she was shanty Irish. She was smart as a whip, razor sharp.

But she was also needy. She was very needy.

Mary Eileen would lay awake at night with David snoring beside her wondering when her Prince Charming would spirit her away from this miserable existence.

Most nights, she fell asleep dreaming about her new love, Hans Mueller. He was a forty-eight-year-old ice cream machinery salesman. If there was anyone in St. Isidore who had an accent thicker than hers, it was Hans .

He was German and never apologized for his ancestry. Like Mary Eileen, he was an immigrant. He had come to St. Isidore because it had such a large German-American population. St. Isidore also had a reputation as a city that welcomed refugees.

And while Hans was anything but a refugee, he sensed that he could build a life here.

Hans wasn't anything special. Yet, he was so much nicer than David. Of course, he was a salesman; it was his job to be nice.

But still, Mary Eileen felt Hans would be a step up from David.

He might not be the prince she dreamed of as her rescuer, but he was still a damn sight better than the lumbering ox who was laying beside her snoring the night away.

And why was he still in her bed anyway?

"You are divorced, aren't you?" Christina asked.

That might seem an intrusive question to be coming from most employees. However, their relationship was more than just that of a boss and an employee. Working as closely as they did for eight to sometimes twelve hours a day, the two women couldn't help but develop a friendship.

Mary Eileen had to admit that what Christina said was true.

They had divorced in 2008. But David refused to move out of their apartment even after Mary Eileen made it clear she was sleeping with a new lover. And there had been several before Hans .

"But he won't go. He just sits up there all day long, while I am working, playing games on that stupid computer of his."

"While you pay for the internet."

"Yes, while I pay for the internet."

"But you are divorced."

"We are divorced."

"Then what the fuck is he still doing in your apartment," Christina said, pointing with one finger toward the ceiling

Mary Eileen didn't say a word. She just smiled and pulled her Beretta out of her purse.

Christina stepped back. Her eyes bulged out of her head and her jaw would have fallen if not for the limits of human anatomy.

Mary Eileen looked to the right and then the left before she brushed Christina's ear with her red lips and whispered, "Maybe I will just kill him."

Both women laughed and shook their heads in unison as the bell on the front door rang announcing new customers.

Three girls had breezed into the Coffee Shoppe with as much carefree energy as only teenagers a few years removed from childhood and a lifetime away from the troubles of being adults could possess.

They bounced and laughed all the way from the front door to the counter ready to order something with enough caffeine and sugar to have them bouncing off the walls.

Mary Eileen turned away from the door so she could slide her pistol back into her purse.

She dreamt about being as happy as those girls, those girls who had never had to walk by soldiers who hated her, who never had to grin and literally bare it for a middle-aged fat man, those girls who didn't have an ex-husband slumping in front of a computer 24/7.

Mary Eileen had never been as happy as those girls. But she would be.

Now as Mary Eileen and Christina finished closing up the Coffee Shoppe for another night, Mary Eileen was happy that she wasn't going home right away this night. That made her feel better. And the thought of what was ahead in the next few hours brightened Mary Eileen's mood even more.

Two

The sound of the Beretta firing, even coming through the heavy ear protection Mary was forced to wear at the St. Isidore Gun & Rod Club, thrilled her.

She was popping round after round at the black outline of a person; the target of a man hanging about ten yards in front of her.

When Mary Eileen emptied her clip, she pushed a button that brought the target up to her face. The sight of the bullet holes was icing on the cake, and just as she did when she finished putting the icing on the coffee cakes at the Coffee Shoppe, Mary Eileen would lick the tip of her tongue across her lip.

It was a special moment.

The targets made it obvious that the class was learning how to shoot at a human being. That bothered some of the other women at first. But it never fazed Mary Eileen Sullivan.

"How can we be expected to shoot at another living, human being?" said one of her classmates, Amanda, about ten years younger than Mary Eileen, a reporter for the local paper, the St. Isidore Chronicle.

That was the same place where David worked, or better put, the Chronicle was his one and only customer for IT work. He probably didn't want any other customers. The Chronicle paid him enough to take care of their social media from his (her) dining room table that he could work two or three hours a day and play games until David collapsed in his (Mary Eileen's) bed.

"This class is about self-defense," Mary Eileen explained. She had noticed Amanda still flinched at the sound of the gunshots on the range. It was not a surprise she had a problem with even the thought of shooting a person.

Mary Eileen sipped from her steaming white chocolate mocha, licking some white cream from her upper lip with the tip of her tongue and set the ceramic mug down softly.

Her blue eyes followed the mug to the thick wooden table top and then rose to meet the questioning eyes of her classmate.

She pushed her thick auburn hair back over her shoulders. Her hair was naturally thick and almost curly but the auburn hue came from a drugstore bottle. Mary Eileen was thinking going back to being an Irish redhead might soon be a good move.

"Don't you wonder what it would be like to actually shoot someone?" Amanda said with a visible shudder. "I couldn't do it. I can even think about it."

"That target is the guy who is trying to rape me or steal from me," Mary Eileen whispered. "And nobody's ever going to do that to me again. That's all I think about."

One round after another. Pop. Pop. Pop. The first three shots went into the body of the targeted silhouette.

"Right where the bastard's heart would be," Mary Eileen whispered to herself.

Pop. Pop. Pop.

The next three went right into the face of her target.

Those shots felt even better.

When she first brought the gun home, still in the box and set it down on the kitchen table, putting the box of ammo she had purchased alongside it; David's eyes had widened.

His slumped shoulders actually squared for a moment. Mary Eileen might have been impressed if it hadn't been for the flesh of his stomach popping out below the t-shirt that was about a size too small for the belly it covered.

David pushed his combed-over hair back in place and patted it down.

They were almost exactly the same age, chronologically, but Mary Eileen felt she was so much older than him in other ways that she had lost respect for David long ago.

“This is what?” he asked rhetorically, sweeping his hand over the table to make sure Mary Eileen knew what he was asking about. It was also a sign that he was in control, still.

Even though she knew David could read as well as she could, Mary Eileen wanted to tell him exactly what was in the boxes. She wanted to say it. Mary Eileen would enjoy every syllable of the answer.

“This is the 21A Beretta Bobcat,” Mary Eileen answered with a smile on her face, sweeping her hand over the table just as David had done a minute before.

“It is user-friendly, durable, reliable and accurate, while with its snag-free lines is can be tucked in any kind of holster or pocket for deep concealment. Available in .22 LR or .25 ACP, it is perfect for concealed carry — on its own or as a backup pistol — and it keeps besting all pistols in its class for quality, value and design,” Mary Eileen said.

None of that was on the box of course. Nor was it original. She had memorized the one-paragraph sales pitch from the company’s website. Mary Eileen had been dreaming about this purchase, for a long time.

David was speechless. His mouth had gone dry. He tried to moisten his lips with his tongue. It only made him seem more useless to Mary Eileen and even less like the man who she could depend on for rescue.

She swept the Beretta and the box of ammo off the table into her large purse and walked out the front door of her, not ‘their,’ apartment, and left David with the grace of a ballerina.

Mary Eileen nearly collapsed when she got down to the alley. She couldn't breathe for a few moments after pulling off the performance of her life. Somehow she had stumbled down the stairs that ran from the apartment’s back door to the alley.

"Oh God, that was good," Mary Eileen said aloud as she opened the back door of the Coffee Shoppe and collapsed inside her tiny office.

After collecting herself, she opened the boxes in her purse, and carefully read the instructions before loading her Beretta.

When she finished, Mary Eileen knew she was locked, loaded and on her way to a new life with Hans.

But first, she had one more class to attend the next night. A local hardware store was giving lessons to women who wanted to learn how to mix and use concrete.

Christina was amazed when Mary Eileen asked her to cover her shift so she could go to that class.

"Why would you ever want to learn that?"

"Repairs, Christina, repairs. I know you have never been down to the cellar. But that is a lot of work to be done," Mary Eileen replied. "And if I can do it myself, I can save a lot of money."

She waved her fingers in the air as she bid Christina farewell for the evening that night, feeling so good about herself.

No one was rescuing Mary Eileen yet. But this was even better. No one needed to save Mary Eileen.

Just like in the days after she landed at LaGuardia, Mary Eileen was solving her problems on her own.

Three

Mary Eileen was happier than she could ever remember being. Well, again, that was not exactly true. She had felt even more wonderful when she landed at LaGuardia.

There were so many people, at the terminal, probably twenty times as many as Mary Eileen might have seen in her village on any day. They were all moving so quickly, too. And they were so loud! How did anyone in New York hear the birds, she would wonder later when she got into the city.

Ah, New York City. If Mary Eileen had been amazed at the crowds, the noise, and the speed at which everything and everyone moved in the airport terminal; she was blasted into a coma when she got off the train at Grand Central Station.

"So this is Grand Central Station," she whispered to herself. Her mother had quite often described their village market as being "busier than Grand Central Station." If her mum had only known how wrong she had been.

The smells! Everyone who brushed by Mary Eileen — and hundreds did— had a different aroma. And they all spoke a different brand of English. Some sounded just like the movie actors Mary Eileen had seen at the cinema. Others had a twang in their voice like the country singers on BBC radio. Still, others were speaking different languages. She lost count at ten different languages, not including all of the different dialects of English.

The noise! It was deafening and thrilling at the same time. Car horns were honking. Truck brakes were squealing. People were talking of course, all very loudly and very quickly. There were musicians on the street, too. Some were playing violins. Other had saxophones. And still, others were playing drums on upside down tin buckets of different shapes and sizes.

Mary Eileen had not felt overpowered by any of it. She simply let herself be swept away into a new life; a life filled with hope.

This morning in St. Isidore she was not feeling quite the same. Not even close, actually. After all, she wasn't the same girl she had been that morning at LaGuardia or that afternoon in Times Square. Now Mary Eileen was no longer a girl. She was a woman. She was, in fact, no matter what David thought he knew, a naturalized American citizen.

Now that had been a proud day in her life. She had only Christina and her customers to share it with, this was long before David, but it had been a happy day, and again a day filled with hope.

This morning had gone wonderfully well. But it was not the great day either of those days had been. Yet, Mary Eileen felt very good. She felt powerful because above all, Mary Eileen Sullivan had hope.

The weather was perfect for coffee. All of her customers had said so. It was the end of summer. The streets of St. Isidore were lined with children playing the last few days before school started, college students from all over the nation who went to schools like Grand Valley State University, and tourists from around the world in town for the annual Art Prize show.

It had been a profitable morning. But it hadn't been perfect. There was a problem with the pipes again.

The plumbing was in terrible shape. The pipes in the stone-walled cellar — it wasn't much more than a cave carved into the stone under the Coffee Shoppe that the locals called a 'Michigan Basement' — had always dripped. Now one of the damn pipes had broken.

Maintenance workers came into the store, and went down into the cellar, then came back upstairs to go back out again for more supplies. There was only one entrance to the cellar. The workers had to go through the store and into the backroom to get to the cellar door. There was no alternative. Customers danced around each other and the workers, trying not to get hit in the head with the long copper pipes being brought in for the repairs.

Oh, the plumbers could have gone through Mary Eileen's office if it hadn't been for the pipes they were carrying and her reluctance to let anyone but Christina into the room that held her safe.

On top of the stream of workers who seemed to get muddier, dirtier and smellier with each trip, there was no way the customers and even the neighbors could miss the noise of the work. The echo of the banging hammers and the howl of metal cutting saws could be heard in the Coffee Shoppe and even out on the street.

But the Coffee Shoppe had been so busy that neither Mary Eileen nor Christina had noticed the time and they got used to the noise. It had been a wonderful morning. They were making some real money for a change.

Mary Eileen caught Christina's eye and smiled. She was happy.

There was a moment the night before when Mary Eileen had wondered if she had made a mistake by telling Christina that she should kill David.

"Damn," she thought. "How could I have said that aloud?"

David was sitting at that stupid computer on the kitchen table, "My computer," Mary Eileen thought bitterly, when she came home from the concrete class at the Home Depot.

She could have strangled him.

David hardly noticed when she walked into the apartment. Just like every hour of every day, he was occupied with one of those idiotic war games, Mary Eileen thought. It's not like he does anything productive. Sure, he does social media for the St. Isidore Chronicle. But after that, he just runs up data and internet charges for useless games.

"I might be shanty Irish," she told Christina, "but he is a typical millennial Momma's boy."

"Probably has a case filled with 'Participation' trophies," Christina said.

As she lay awake beside David—"What is he doing in my bed?" Mary Eileen thought—thinking about Hans. He had been in the Coffee Shoppe during the day. He wasn't pitching new ice cream machinery this time. Hans just sat at the counter listening to Mary tell him about growing up in Ireland and then what it was like moving to America.

During a lull in business, Mary Eileen caught Christina's attention, winked and got a wink back. That meant Christina would cover for her while she and Hans snuck out to his car and made love in the back seat of her Volvo. It wasn't the first time it had happened, and it was never really like making love.

"It was more like making lust," Mary Eileen had admitted to Christina after the first time. But it was the best she'd had in a long time.

Hans listened to me. He talked to me. And he turned me on, Mary Eileen thought, laying awake while David snored.

Hans cares about me.

If only Hans was laying beside me, she thought.

But the slumbering, snoring, waste of humanity beside her wasn't Hans. It was David.

That was a depressing thought. But it could be worse. At least she had hope.

Her plan was coming together. But Mary Eileen was worried that she might have tipped her hand to Christina. It was one thing to enlist her as a co-conspirator in slipping out the back for a quick roll in the Volvo, It was something else to talk about killing someone.

But then again, it's not like they didn't live in the United States of America where people get shot every day. And, sometimes, they just disappeared.

Mary Eileen read about it all the time. And her customers talked about it, too. Husbands and wives were always disappearing from one another. In this day and age, it isn't any problem to just walk away, Mary Eileen thought.

And with so many people in this country, in the state of Michigan and in this city of St. Isidore; who is going to miss just one more who disappears. It's not like there won't be another person to take his place.

And with that thought, she fell asleep.

In the morning, the sunlight was streaming through her bedroom window. Mary Eileen was alone. She touched herself and found she was damp. Mary Eileen had been dreaming about Hans and making wild love to him.

With a contented sigh, she rolled over on her side and tried to go back to the dream, or at least to recapture the exquisite feeling of warm lust that had overtaken her.

Then she heard David banging on the keyboard of her, yes her, computer. Mary rolled on her stomach and shoved her face into a pillow in an effort to escape.

But the only real way to get away was to run to the bathroom, get in the shower, grab some coffee and toast, and go to work.

David grunted at her as she went by. Mary Eileen was glad he did no more than that. The other day he'd reached around and slapped her butt. That was a morning when she just about lost it.

Her Beretta was in her purse and she was as locked and loaded as the weapon.

Four

The people of St. Isidore liked to think of themselves as residents of a big city. One of the radio stations did traffic reports only because a survey showed their listeners, even though they never had to wait through more than one red light at any intersection, would feel more "big city" if they listened to traffic reports on the radio. But St. Isidore wasn't Detroit and it sure as hell wasn't New York.

Mary Eileen laughed to herself when she thought about these people in St. Isidore dealing with the kind of crime and murder she had seen growing up in Dublin or even during her relatively brief stay in New York.

Murder in St. Isidore? A dozen or so people got killed every year. But nobody thought it could happen to them, at least her customers didn't. And Mary Eileen would be willing to bet none of her customers thought seriously about pulling the trigger on someone else's life.

But murder was on Mary Eileen's mind.

How else was she going to rid herself of David, who was not only occupying her apartment and monopolizing her computer; he was also sleeping in her bed.

"You know I am fucking around on you, right?" Mary Eileen had said to him more than a month ago.

He snored.

"David, I don't love you," Mary Eileen said, straddling his body, shaking his shoulders to wake him up. "I do not love you."

"Is it your time of the month, already?"

"You are walking on thin ice."

"Me? What about you? What would you do without me?"

Just as the answer "Be happy," sprung into her mind, Mary Eileen realized with a shudder that David was actually getting excited. She was straddling him and had made the mistake of putting her body directly on top of his cock.

David was growing harder by the second. Mary Eileen, revolted as she was by the sight of this sleeping goon under her was getting wet. After all, there was a time when he turned her on. And she was still excited by him. David had made her feel special, loved, everything a woman wanted.

He put his hands on her shoulders and started moving her back and forth and then around in small circles on his hard cock.

"David, stop it," she said, her breathing betraying her excitement. It was fun being on top.

He didn't answer. He just slid inside and started thrusting.

"Oh, fuck it," Mary Eileen whispered.

"Yeah, oh yeah," said David.

It was over in a few minutes. Mary Eileen came out of the bathroom to find David snoring, again. God, how she hated that.

"You know I am sleeping with Hans."

There, I said it, Mary Eileen thought. Might as well get it out.

David snored.

Mary Eileen took one of his nipples in her fingers and twisted hard.

"Ow! Goddamn, woman!"

"I said, 'I am sleeping with Hans'"

"I know."

"You know, and you are still here?"

"We are divorced, right? What's wrong with playing around? We can be friends, right?"

"What the fuck? What did we just do?"

"That was just one of the benefits of friendship," said David.

Oh, my God, Mary Eileen thought, as David rolled away from her. There is no end to this, is there?

Wait a minute, she thought. It was an epiphany that came with an extra shot of espresso, a bolt of energy. Mary Eileen sat up in bed.

If he doesn't care if I am sleeping with Hans, who is David sleeping with?

"You, motherfucker," Mary Eileen said as she grabbed her pillows, pulled a blanket out of the cedar chest and stormed off for another night on the couch.

"THIS IS ALL ABOUT YOU, isn't it?" Mary Eileen said the next morning to David's back while he worked on some stupid social media stuff for the St. Isidore Chronicle.

Good god, what a slug, she thought. Sits around on that fat ass all day, never has to deal with a customer, sometimes I am the only human being he speaks with all day. Take a shower, fat ass.

David kind of waved his hand back at her but didn't bother to answer. He didn't have to. Mary Eileen knew she was right.

David's self-obsession and stubbornness went beyond refusing to leave his ex-wife's apartment and bed.

He didn't even seem to care, that Mary Eileen had a gun, a Beretta pistol. She should have expected it. David loved guns. His guns were laying all over the apartment. Pistols, revolvers, even rifles, and shotguns. The idea that Mary Eileen was packing a gun in her purse, after the time she surprised him with it, never crossed his mind again. But it might have if David had known Mary Eileen had signed-up for marksmanship lessons at the St. Isidore Gun & Rod Club.

She was learning how to use the Beretta. Better yet, she was not just learning how to shoot the gun; Mary Eileen was taking target practice with the weapon. Amanda and the rest of her fellow students would have told David that she was getting pretty damn good at it too if he had bothered to ask, or to even join them at one of their coffee get-togethers after class.

Wouldn't all of that set off alarm bells in most ex-husbands, especially ex-husbands who had to know they weren't welcome?

Mary Eileen even joked with Christina once about how she was going to use the pistol to kill David. But, then again, if David had learned about that it could have smoothed over any suspicions he might have been having. After all, what killer was going to tell her murderous plan to a friend if she was going to evict him with a Dear David slug from a Beretta? She must have been kidding or PMS-ing David must have decided.

He would have been wrong. Nothing separates a couple like death. And that's all Mary Eileen could think about even while she was at work.

The rage simmered in Mary Eileen, turning her into a human pressure cooker. It's one thing to decide to kill someone in a moment of passion or a flash of white-hot anger and then not act on the impulse.

But when rage simmers, boiling up some days, down on other days, but always there; it can motivate a person to do almost anything.

"If he leaves, we can be together," Hans had told her more than once.

"You will move in?"

"We can marry."

"Really?"

"Yes, really," Hans answered as he actually dropped to one knee the last time they had had this discussion.

"Please say you will be mine forever," he said. "Please let me make you happy."

Mary Eileen wanted to be happy. She wanted to be with Hans. Everything she wanted was on the other side of David.

Five

Three days after Hans promised his undying love, Mary Eileen decided that she had had enough. The pipes were broken in the cellar again. The water pressure was so low it was tough to get even a simple cup of coffee brewed.

The maintenance guys tracked mud all over the Coffee Shoppe. She and Christina had spent three hours after closing mopping it all up.

"We clean up their shit, and still I have to pay them for the pleasure of the experience," Mary Eileen said as she and Christina sweated.

That was another thing. The air conditioning wasn't working well. So that meant more repairmen and more repair bills.

God this life sucks, Mary Eileen thought they next day as she pushed a loose strand of her thick, auburn hair way from her face.

It had been a rough morning. She decided it was time to go home for lunch. Just as Mary Eileen stepped out of the door and into the alley, the sky burst open.

Spring had laid out its welcome mat early in St. Isidore a couple of days ago. It had been unseasonably warm, very pleasant actually. The snow and ice left over from a brutal winter had melted creating little rivers to wash the streets clean.

But then it rained. It poured. And it was more than rain. Winter wasn't ready to release St. Isidore from its ugly grasp. Some snow, sleet and ice came down with the rain.

Mary Eileen was more what soaking wet.

She was soaking miserable.

Mary Eileen walked down the alley behind the Coffee Shoppe, and then up the stairs to the apartment that she was unwillingly sharing with David a day longer, with a splash. At least two inches of water were in her boots. Her feet were soaked.

And then Mary Eileen saw David where he always was; at the kitchen table doing something — maybe working or maybe playing games — on the computer.

She didn't snap. She didn't act on impulse. She simply boiled over.

Mary Eileen pulled the Beretta out of her purse and fired three shots into the back of his head.

David's skull exploded onto the computer. A warm backwash of brains, blood, and bits of skull landed on Mary Eileen. That was a shock. It woke her up to the reality of what she had just done.

The mess was something she had not counted on. Now she was afraid. Her fear would only get worse.

Suddenly she realized it was 3 p.m. Children were outside playing. People were walking to and from the shops on the street; one of those quaint, old-style European streets built before automobiles. Although many of the buildings were constructed with thick brick walls, there could still be very few secrets, especially the secrets of three shots fired into the back of a man's head.

And here was Mary Eileen with David's dead body on her dining room table.

What should she do now? No matter how much housework a person might be accustomed to it can't compare to cleaning up the mess left by a dead body, especially a corpse with its brains splattered across a dining room table.

Mary Eileen washed David's blood, flesh, brains, and tiny bits of skull off her hands and her forearms. There were splashes of blood and whatever else flew backward on her face and neck as well.

Mary Eileen decided washing up after a homicide is something that is never described accurately enough on TV crime shows.

Just as she got herself clean, Mary Eileen's smartphone rang.

Good God, she thought, is it a neighbor who heard the gunshots?

If so, how would she explain the noise? And what if someone knocked at the door to make sure she and David are okay. Certainly, she was not going to be able to move his corpse, and whoever was standing in the door of the apartment would be able to look over her head and see David's body.

It was a corpse, by the way, that was already starting to smell.

The phone rang again.

Fuck. Maybe it was Cheryl next door. Did she hear the gunshots?

Mary Eileen ran over to the TV, desperately searching for a cowboy or police show that could be used to explain the sounds of gunfire.

She found one turned up the volume and only then picked up her smartphone, held her breath, and answered.

It was Sue Ann, one of the college kids Mary Eileen hired to get through spring break and the tourist season.

Guess what? A busload of tourists had just unloaded in front of the Coffee Shoppe.

"Can you come back, please? It's a bunch of old people on their way down to the Tulip Time thing in Holland. Some of them are even asking for something called, 'Sanka.' Everybody wants decaf," Sue Ann said.

Thank God, Mary Eileen thought.

She had never been so relieved to be needed at the Coffee Shoppe. This was one time she would not complain about someone on the staff asking for assistance.

The sound of the bus and its air brakes, along with those old people all yelling at each other to be heard probably covered the sounds of the gunshots.

So that was all good.

But Mary Eileen looked back at David's body on the table. That was bad.

What was she going to do about him? Getting David to move out of the apartment was tough enough before Mary Eileen squeezed the trigger. Now her dilemma had increased exponentially. What was she to do?

The decision would have to wait.

She turned to look at him one last time and left David where he lay, on her dining room table.

Six

When Mary Eileen returned from the Coffee Shoppe, she cleaned. Mary Eileen spent the first hours of the night washing and disinfecting the dining room. Then she moved through the rest of the apartment, just in case she had tracked traces of blood or brain into the other rooms. All the while, she was looking at David's body, wondering how she was going to get rid of it.

Well, it didn't take a master criminal to realize she had to get the body out of the apartment. Mary Eileen needed a plan.

She was not a large woman. And David was not a small man. Mary Eileen would learn the truth of the expression "dead weight" this night.

She pushed and pulled his corpse off the dining room table. It hit the floor was a wet thud as more brain and blood came out of his head. There was a rather small entrance wound at the back of his skull. But at least a third of his face seemed to have been blown off by the exit wound.

More mess to clean, Mary Eileen realized.

That would have to wait.

She put her arms under David's armpits and started dragging him backward. Again, more mess as his body left a skid mark of death on the floor that she had already cleaned and disinfected.

Mary Eileen was able to get the body out of the apartment through the back door. After catching her breath and wiping the sweat from her face, she started dragging David down the stairs.

It was a peaceful night in the neighborhood. A cat could be heard meowing and a small dog was barking, but those sounds were nothing out of the ordinary.

The only sound that was truly extraordinary, Mary Eileen realize was the noise of her ex-husband's dead body bumping and thumping i way down the wood steps of the staircase that went from her apartmen to the ground.

Mary Eileen cringed with every thud and waited for a neighbor t poke his or her head out of a bedroom window to find out what w making the sound of a wet sack of cement bouncing off wood.

Finally she hit the bottom step and was able to pull David's corp to her car.

Oh, Lord! If dragging her dead ex-husband off the dining roo table, through the apartment and then down the stairs had required e traordinary strength from this average-sized woman, superhuman mu cles would be needed to lift the body into the trunk of her car.

Taking David for his final drive into the country to dump his boc had been Plan 'A" for Mary Eileen. She thought of it while working c her books at the Coffee Shoppe. But she never expected it would l next to impossible for her to lift the body up off the ground and in the trunk.

Plan 'A' wasn't going to work. She had no time for a 'Plan B.' Ma Eileen had made enough noise to wake the living about the reality of dead man in the neighborhood. Besides, she had to get cleaned up ar go to work.

There was nothing else to do but to push and drag David into storage shed. She closed the shed door as quietly as she could and the went back up to her apartment.

Mary Eileen showered after doing her best to quickly erase the sk marks of death from her floor and tried to get some sleep.

Every muscle in her body, including those she didn't know existe ached so loudly that Mary Eileen was nearly screaming in agony. Hov ever, the last thing she wanted to do was to call any attention to herse So she would put in a full day at the Coffee Shoppe.

But only half her mind would be on her customers and employee

The other half would be occupied with trying to come up with 'Plan B.' What was she going to do with David's body? But that was only half of the problem facing her that day, and Mary Eileen knew it.

But first things, first, she had to dispose of the body. However, there was something even more important to do, and that was to get some sleep.

THE NEXT DAY, MARY Eileen decided to burn David's corpse. It was not an easy decision. She spent the day serving ice cream, paying bills, dealing with Christina and the other employees, and dreading the first time someone asked, "Hey, how is David doing?" or even worse; they might ask, "Is David upstairs?"

Those were two questions Mary Eileen did not want to face. So as soon as it got dark, she went back to work on disposing of this ex-husband of hers. Ironically, Mary Eileen was having as much trouble getting rid of his corpse as she had to get her ex out of the apartment.

When it was dark, she dragged the body out of the storage shed and into a yard behind her building. Moving David wasn't as hard as it had been. She developed a system and a rhythm to get up under his body and use her body as kind of a sled to pull it across the broken concrete of the alley and into the yard.

Now it was time to light David's funeral pyre. She covered the corpse with branches and leaves, found some old newspapers crumpled the pages and tossed them on the pile. Anything to serve as kindling she figured had to help. Mary Eileen poured gasoline over it all and lit a match.

Good, God! The pile exploded. It was all she could do to jump out of the way. Thank heavens she had been standing back when she tossed the match. As soon as it hit the fumes of the gasoline — maybe she had gone overboard on the gas — the flames erupted.

She was breathing heavy. This felt good. Mary Eileen probably should have worried about the smell of burning flesh. How would she explain that to the neighbors?

But on this city block, what with the homeless wandering like zombies all night long talking to the traffic lights, there was always an odd assortment of odors.

At least she hoped that would be an explanation that would be accepted if a neighbor couldn't help but stick his or her nose where it did not belong.

Mary Eileen went back to her apartment. If someone did come along to investigate the fire, she didn't want to be at the scene of the crime.

So, she went back upstairs and waited.

Mary Eileen thought about showering to wash away the stench of David's corpse —burning it didn't come a moment too soon — but decided she might as well wait.

When she went outside with a shovel and a dust pan, Mary Eileen figured cleaning up the ashes would be the easiest part of this disposal job, she nearly cried.

David's corpse had not been reduced to ashes. It had not even been burnt beyond recognition. The body had only been singed.

Now Mary Eileen needed a 'Plan C.' She was too tired to even think about that as she dragged the body, which smelled even worse now, back to the storage shed.

Seven

St. Isidore tended to be a cloudy, rainy city. It wasn't too unlike the British Isles in that regard, Mary Eileen thought. So when she awoke the next morning at 6 am to sunshine coming through her bedroom window, that was a bonus.

However, the moment of euphoria disappeared when she took her first deep breath. The odor of disinfectant and bleach hung in the apartment.

"Good God, it's worse than a swimming pool that's overdosing on chlorine," Mary Eileen said aloud. Then she glanced quickly to the left and the right to make sure the ghost of David had not heard her.

He had not been such a bad guy, that David. Maybe he just couldn't help himself. Mary Eileen knew she had killer's remorse. But at the same time, she had to admit that maybe the murder of David had been a mistake. After all, there had been a time when she loved him. Or at least Mary Eileen thought she had loved him.

Yes, I did love him, she thought. I did love him. But he let me down. He didn't make me happy. And face it, there was no way that St. Isidore boy was going to move out of this city. None of them every does.

Oh yes, Mary Eileen knew this city.

Mary Eileen had not met more than one or two people in St. Isidore who could honestly be described as "friendly." There was always kind of a film over them, an air of self-righteous arrogance that passed for being nice.

The city had been overwhelmingly Dutch from the late 1700s through the mid-to-late twentieth century; Mary Eileen had heard the town's favorite expression then had always been, "If you ain't Dutch, you ain't much." It didn't ring as true anymore. But it could have been replaced with "If you weren't born here, you'll never be much."

St. Isidore natives could be friendly, but they could never be your friend if you weren't born and raised here. Mary Eileen had learned that early on. And David was a native. So maybe he couldn't help himself, she thought, pulling the covers up around her neck.

When her fingers got near her nose, Mary Eileen could still smell David. Or better put, she could smell the stench of his rotting corpse.

"Oh my God!" Mary Eileen screamed as she jumped out of bed, getting her legs and feet tangled in the comforter, ruining her exit.

Mary Eileen screamed and cried, literally bawled like a baby, as she fought to get out of the tangled web she had woven in her bed. It all came out. All the tension. All the guilt. Oh sweet Jesus, what have I done?

Mary Eileen fell out of the bed, landing flat on her stomach. She slowly pulled herself up to her knees and prayed at the side of the bed like she had not done since childhood.

She wept the tears of a woman who had killed for the first time. Mary Eileen had quite often considered murder as an option. And there were very few mornings that she hadn't thought about suicide as a viable option. And she knew the latter was just as sinful as the former.

But now, Mary Eileen had done it. There was no turning back. Was she doomed to Hell?

Wouldn't you know it? Church bells began to ring out. Oh, my God, Mary Eileen thought, her breath catching in her throat. Her racing heart came to a sudden stop.

Just as quickly Mary Eileen began to laugh. It is Sunday, she thought, of course, church bells are ringing. There are hundreds of churches in this city and scores of them are downtown. Why wouldn't I hear church bells?

Mary Eileen laughed so hard, with such violent relief, that she began to cry again. But it was the tears of a happy woman running down her cheeks.

She sat down on the floor and thought this through.

"David deserved to die," Mary Eileen said aloud so that she would hear it and believe it.

"He was the one who promised we would move out of this little city. He was the one who promised to at least visit Ireland with me. He was the one who pledged to make me happy," she said. "He was the one who failed."

Mary Eileen padded barefoot across the wood floor of her bedroom into the kitchen and poured some coffee beans into the grinder.

"I promised to love him until death did us part," she said with a smile and pushed the button to grind the beans.

"Guess what motherfucker," Mary Eileen said, underlining every syllable of the sentence with her thickest Irish brogue, "we are apart."

Relaxing with her first cup of coffee, realizing it was Sunday and she had the whole day ahead of her, Mary Eileen sat in her breakfast nook, looked out the window and said to herself, "I got you out of my apartment finally. Now I just need to get you out of that goddamn storage shed."

Mary Eileen realized she was only kidding herself. Getting the body out of the shed was the easiest of the chores that lay ahead of her.

Once it was out, what was she going to do with the corpse?

While she thought and worked on her second cup of the day, one of Mary Eileen's neighbors supplied the answer as he used a chain saw to cut through some branches that had fallen in last week's windstorm.

She eased out of her wooden breakfast nook chair and walked to the window, peeking out through the curtains like she was afraid of being spotted.

"That's it!" Mary Eileen whispered. "How hard can that be?"

DRIVING BACK HOME WITH the chainsaw in the trunk of her Volvo, Mary Eileen felt like a genuinely empowered woman. She pushed the car through its five-speeds, smoothly sliding the stick to her right from one gear to the next, effortless controlling the engine with perfect hand-eye-left-foot-right-foot-coordination.

For the first time in a long time, Mary Eileen felt like she was actually in control of her life. There would be no more kowtowing to David, worrying about sounding "too Irish" for his St. Isidorian friends.

God, what a basketful of morons these idiots are, Mary Eileen thought, not worrying for a moment about how she would explain David's absence.

"Should be easy," Mary Eileen said aloud as she downshifted to third gear to take a hairpin curve on the exit ramp from U-S. 131 to I-196 before sliding the stick down to fourth to accelerate as she came out of the curve.

"I'll just tell them that David left," Mary Eileen said, hoping she could produce a tear or two to dribble down her cheeks, "and I have absolutely no idea where he could be."

They'll believe it all, Mary Eileen thought as she came off the expressway and prepared to take a right turn on red without touching her brake. Sure handed, with total confidence, she downshifted to second the engine powered down and then she accelerated as she popped it into third, flew over a mini-mogul in the crappy pavement on College Avenue and screamed into a hard left-hand turn onto Michigan Street

A five-speed saved my life, Mary Eileen thought before getting back to the matter at hand.

"They'll believe it all," she said aloud, laying out the next step in her plan to be free forever.

"They'll believe it all because they want to believe it," Mary Eileen said with a smile for the rear-view mirror, winking a green eye at the dimple on the left side of her mouth.

"Whenever you want a lie to be believed, just tell them what they really want to hear, and they'll buy it every time," she said with a laugh as she idled into the garage that doubled as a storage shed for the Coffee Shoppe.

Eight

David's body was way too heavy for a woman the size of Mary Eileen to move on her own. She certainly could not ask anyone for help. But as soon as she heard her neighbor's chainsaw the answer blazed in her mind like the neon sign that told her customers the Coffee Shoppe was open for business.

She had the body. Now she had the chainsaw.

All Mary Eileen had to do was cut off David's head, arms, and legs and then stuff the body parts into the cellar. Nobody ever went down into the basement except she and the maintenance workers who had to fix the decades-old plumbing system. The pipes were always leaking and sometimes breaking. So there was a chance of discovery. But Mary Eileen couldn't let that get in the way of her plan. After all, what other choice was there?

Chopping up a human body with a chain saw was not as easy as she thought, or hoped it would be. Just pulling the cord to start the machine was a challenge. When the chain started ripping into David's body, blood flew everywhere. Even four days after his death, fluids were in his corpse, and they all came out.

Mary Eileen found herself in a scene from a horror movie. Blood, flesh, and bone fragments flew into the air, coating her face and becoming entwined in her hair. The noise was even worse. The sound of the saw and the grinding sound it made when the chain of blades hit bone bounced off the stone walls right back at Mary Eileen.

But she kept at it. Finally, she had David in several manageable pieces. Lying at her feet were a head, two legs, two arms and a torso.

Mary Eileen was soaked with her sweat and David's bodily fluids. She might have even peed herself. Her jeans were such a wet, soaked mess that Mary Eileen couldn't be sure. But her work was not finished. Now she had to get rid of the body parts.

The next night, she came back with a bag of concrete, a wheelbarrow and a hose that she ran down from a faucet on the side of the building.

She mixed concrete for each body part, poured it into metal tubs. Then she added the arms, legs, and head to their own individual tubs. Mary Eileen carried the metal buckets that contained the pieces of David farther back into the cellar and stashed them with the rocks, stones and other junk that had been piled up over the decades.

Mary Eileen was getting better at anticipating the challenges faces a murderess. Thinking ahead, she also brought air fresheners with her to hang and hide the smell of David.

Outside, it was dark. Pitch black. Mary Eileen stripped naked in the backyard and set her wet clothes on fire. It was like an appalling part of her life was going up in smoke along with her jeans and t-shirt. She even burned her shoes and socks. All of it went up in flames.

Back upstairs in her apartment, which smelled so fricking clean now, she couldn't believe it; Mary Eileen turned the shower on as hot as she could stand it and thought about what would have to happen next.

She would have to tell two lies to finish the coverup.

"WELL, DAVID'S GONE," Mary Eileen announced as she breezed through the front door of the Coffee Shoppe the next morning.

"What?" Christina said. "Oh no!"

She felt for Mary Eileen. Even though David was a total jerk, nobody liked to be dumped. It was okay to be the dumper, but never the dumpee. And Mary Eileen was obviously hurting. Her eyes were as red as if she had been up all night crying and the bags under her eyes were carrying luggage.

Christina moved to Mary Eileen's side, put one arm around her shoulders and used her free hand to rub her back.

"About time," said Jack, one of the regulars at the Coffee Shoppe who had spent the past month falling asleep with a tall coffee cooling on the table beside the overstuffed chair that was his second home.

"I don't believe it," Amanda whispered to Joy, her partner in crime reporting at the St. Isidore Chronicle.

Joy heard but didn't care. She just wanted to get her two coffees and get back to the Chronicle. The newspaper was her second home, and oh yeah, the two coffees? She would down both by the time she and Amanda hit their desks.

"What? Who?" Joy whispered back.

"Her ex," Amanda said. "They got divorced I don't know how long ago. But he never moved out."

"Wow," said Joy. "There's a guy who is totally illiterate when it comes to reading the writing on the wall."

"He just left?" Christina said.

"Packed his bags. Gone for good, I hope," said Mary Eileen.

"Everything's gone?"

Oh crap, Mary Eileen thought to herself. Everything was not gone. Damn! David's clothes were still in the closet. His stuff was still in the bathroom, shampoo, and all that crap. Damn!

"Uh, yeah," Mary Eileen stammered while making a note to herself about scheduling another late night open-pit fire in the alley.

"I guess he finally got the message," Jack said as he picked his book back up and started reading again about Hitler's invasion of France.

The curtain came down on Act One.

The next day, after taking three showers to wash the smell of smoke out off her body and out of her nose, Mary Eileen called in sick for the morning.

"I just can't do it," she whispered to Christina, choking up as she spoke a sentence she'd been rehearsing for the past hour.

"Don't worry," Christina said. "We can cover for you."

"Thanks!"

Amanda and Joy looked at Christina with eyes open and accepting, should she choose to share.

Christina took a deep, dramatic breath and said, "The poor woman is still hurting. She could barely talk."

If Mary Eileen had heard what her favorite employee had announced to the customers at Coffee Shoppe, she would have laughed and noted she was half right.

Well, maybe close to eighty percent correct. Mary Eileen's back and arms were a little sore from carrying all of David's crap out for the 2 a.m. alley bonfire. So she was hurting.

"And, yeah, I am having trouble talking," Mary Eileen might have said. "Next time I'll wash the cinnamon scone down with some coffee before I try to say anything."

Always an accomplished actress — and a real trooper who could play through her pain — Mary Eileen burst into tears that afternoon while working on the books in her office at the Coffee Shoppe.

As one giant, caring mass of humanity; her employees and customers, who let themselves into her office thanks to a conveniently open door, put their arms around Mary Eileen to console her and remind her that she was well rid of David.

Hearing that, Mary Eileen couldn't help but smile through her tears and nod in agreement. She bit her lip too. Everybody thought she was trying to hold back more sobs.

But in truth, was just hoping the door to the cellar, which was just down the hall from her office, was closed and locked tight.

"You are right," she said, "thank God, David's gone!"

She stood to break the group hug — a little of this sympathy was going a long way, and she was having trouble holding back a laugh — and everyone backed off.

"We need to go back to work," Mary Eileen said with a sniff. "Life goes on, right?"

"Life always goes on," said Amanda.

"At least for most of us," Mary Eileen said to herself.

"What?" Christina said.

"Oh, nothing, nothing," Mary Eileen said, choking back another sob and covering her mouth with her hand to hide the beginnings of a smile.

Christina looked at her with a new respect a couple of hours later when the after-work crowd hit the Coffee Shoppe. Mary Eileen kept her head up the whole time. She is laughing and smiling when she must be a mess inside, Christina thought.

Mary Eileen was laughing at that moment when Cheryl, the neighbor who ran the boutique dress shop next door and, like Mary Eileen, lived in an apartment above her business, asked about the noise she heard the other night.

"It sounded like a chainsaw," Cheryl said. "What were you doing over there?"

"Oh, nothing, really. I just got a new coffee grinder in and was trying it out before I took it downstairs."

"At 1 a.m.?"

"So, sorry to wake you," Mary Eileen said, while she wondered how tough it would be to shoot this bitch in the back of the head and add her to the body shop in the cellar.

"Won't happen again, I guarantee it."

Nine

Mary Eileen could imagine what they were saying. She could almost hear them talking.

"Where is David?" one customer might ask another.

"I don't know," another would answer. "I haven't seen him in a month."

"Do you really think he just vanished?"

"Do you really think she expects us to believe that?"

Mary Eileen knew that sometimes there was a difference between being paranoid and being correct.

"They are all talking about us," Mary Eileen mumbled to herself.

"I'm sorry," said Amanda. "What?"

Mary Eileen blinked and fell back a step from the counter. Amanda, the reporter from the Chronicle that she knew from their gun class, had said something. Mary Eileen felt as stupid as she had in school when she was living in some fantasy world in her mind rather than paying attention to the teacher.

"No, I am the one who should be sorry," Mary Eileen said with a laugh, putting on the brogue, playing the Irish clown. "I am terribly sorry, Joy. What was it you wanted?"

"Amanda."

"Oh, of course, Amanda,"

Damn! Mary Eileen thought. Gotta get back up to speed her. Rejoin reality.

"I just need two large coffees and one regular."

"All for you?" Mary Eileen laughed. She was recovering. "Oh, now, I see Joy."

"Hi, Joy," Mary Eileen called out waving her fingers in greeting when she spotted Joy, sitting at a table by the window.

Boy, she's been putting on weight, Mary Eileen thought.

"You both look so good," she said, "you and Joy. Everything going all right at the paper?"

"Oh yes, about as good as ever," Amanda said, pausing before she went in for the kill.

"How are you doing? I understand David left. I am so sorry."

Amanda putting her fingers on the back of Mary Eileen's hand that was resting on the counter, a hand that Mary Eileen snatched back like she'd been touched by a red-hot spider.

"Yes, fine, well..." Mary Eileen hadn't been ready for this. But she did her best to summon tears on command, again.

"I wouldn't ask. I would never dream of prying," Amanda said with half a smile, "but the thing is, David hasn't been to work in a couple of weeks. We are all very anxious."

"Well, I am worried too, " Mary Eileen stammered. "I mean I had no clue that he was going to leave. I haven't heard from him either."

"Well, if you hear anything..."

"Oh yes...

"Anything at all..."

"Anything at all," Mary Eileen said, "any word at all, and I will let you folks at the Chronicle know right away."

"Thanks," Amanda said with a wink as she managed to hold three coffee cups between her hands and walked back to her table.

As soon as Amanda's back was turned, Mary Eileen nearly fainted. She put a hand down on the counter to steady herself and looked out the window. She glanced down a few inches and saw Joy's smiling face looking back at her.

"Oh, hi again," Mary Eileen mouthed silently.

She turned her back to the window as Joy got out of her chair to help Amanda.

AMANDA WAS QUIVERING when she got back to the table. Her hands were trembling so badly that drops of coffee were spilling out of the cups she was barely managing to hang on to as Joy rose from her chair.

"Here, give me those," Joy said as she tried to prevent what could be a bath of hot coffee.

Just as she got up, some moron outside started honking at another motorist taking too long to move from the traffic light on the corner of DeVos Avenue and Butterworth Street. Amanda jumped at the sound of the horn. Joy overreacted and the scalding hot coffee that the Coffee Shoppe was famous for splashed onto her forearm.

"Goddamn, it girl!"

"Sorry, boss."

Joy and Amanda smiled at each other and took deep breaths before seating down without further loss of coffee or skin.

Joy looked over Amanda's shoulder as she licked her wrist where the coffee had splattered. She locked eyes with Mary Eileen who seemed unable to shift her gaze from the Chronicle reporters sitting by the window that served as the Coffee Shoppe's eye on DeVos Avenue.

Joy decided she wasn't going to be the first to blink and she wasn't

As tough as Mary Eileen was, moving alone to the U.S. from Ireland, finding her way in New York and then starting her own business in St. Isidore — she had met her match in Joy Ellis.

After all, Joy, and Amanda too, had made their names in St. Isidore by tracking down a serial killer. They had not captured him, nor had they freed the women he was holding. But they had found his lair, his dungeon, and that was more than anyone had ever done for the women who were always disappearing in St. Isidore.

So neither of them were about to be frightened by Mary Eileen Sullivan.

Mary Eileen blinked first. A customer had distracted her. But as soon as she could, she returned to watching Joy and Amanda.

Now the two women were locked in an animated and heated discussion, both whispering intensely, worrying Mary Eileen even more.

"Incoming," Christina said as she gently nudged her boss and nodded her head toward the front door. A busload of Suicide Forest tourists was unloading.

"More deadies," Christina said, referring to the people that came from around the world to visit St. Isidore's Suicide Forest, the place where the world came to die. These people would probably go home alive, Mary Eileen thought. They were just there to see if they could find some corpses swinging in the trees.

It was disgusting and ghoulish, but also highly profitable for the merchants of St. Isidore. So, Mary Eileen had to attend to the fanny-packed senior citizens who were dying for a coffee and sweet roll before they began their search for the dead in earnest.

But Mary Eileen was not able to give them her full attention. She happened to glance up and over the shoulder of one of the tourists in time to see Joy and Amanda trying to work their way through the mob.

Joy looked back. Her eyes locked on to Mary Eileen. The owner of the Coffee Shoppe realized she had a new problem.

Ten

Esther had taken over the St. Isidore Chronicle publisher's office from her father about a year ago, and the first thing she had done was to move Joy, Amanda and their staff of six interns out of the basement office that served as a base of operations for their first missing person quest.

It was in this new brick-walled, airy, timber-ceiling office that Amanda and Joy landed after the morning visit to the Coffee Shoppe.

"So how do we begin?" Amanda asked Joy.

"It's settled in your mind? We need to look for David Van Holt?"

"Yes, I can feel it. Mary Eileen is not being honest with us. She's..."

"Proof is what we need. Suspicion is excellent, but proving it. That's the challenge," Joy reminded Amanda as she got up from behind her slick, chrome desk that had replaced the wooden monstrosity no one could lug out of the old basement office.

"Is anyone else looking for David? Has a missing person report been filed with the St. Izzy police," Joy asked with a tone that always got under Amanda's thin skin.

There was nothing Amanda hated more than rhetorical questions. Joy knew the answer to everything she had asked.

"Isn't there something to be said for a reporter's intuition?" Amanda said. "Besides, I've shot guns with this woman. I am more than a customer."

Joy needed coffee. She'd gone through her two large Coffee Shoppe cups. It was time for another round. She got up to go down the hall to the employee kitchenette, thinking Amanda would take the hint.

She didn't.

"I am close to her, and I could get closer," Amanda said, walking as fast as she could to keep up with Joy so she could put her face in front of the galloping coffee hound to get her boss' full attention.

It wasn't that Joy thought Amanda was wrong. She had read the guilt in Mary Eileen's face. When their eyes had locked, it was like a mutual electric shock had passed through the women.

Joy had no doubt Amanda was right. Something was wrong at the Coffee Shoppe. There was something mysterious about David's disappearance.

But Joy also believed in hedging her bets. It would be one thing to discover David had disappeared without a trace. It was quite another challenge to find him dead or alive especially without putting themselves in harm's way. She didn't want to launch into a wild goose chase with no chance of success.

Joy also didn't want to get either she or Amanda killed. What her headstrong, quite attractive and very talented protege failed to realize was that if Mary Eileen did have something to do with David Van Holt's disappearance, she might want to keep her role in that mystery quiet.

And if Mary Eileen had killed once, she might be willing to do it again.

"Let's say, just for the sake of argument that you are right. We know David is gone. Mary Eileen said he just picked up his stuff and left. She was as surprised as any of us. Let's say there is something more to it. Let's say she had something to do with his disappearance..."

"Exactly what I am thinking."

"I know what you are thinking. But what I am thinking has not occurred to you, I am afraid. Let's go crazy on this and say that, God forbid, Mary Eileen Sullivan killed David Van Holt."

"You think?"

Jesus, it is like trying to tame a wild filly every time Amanda gets on one of her journalistic missions, Joy thought.

"No, I don't believe that, right now. I don't have any proof of that at all. I don't have one iota of evidence and neither do you. We suspect something is going on over there. But we have no proof."

"Well, how are we going to get proof if we don't investigate," Amanda said with her arms crossed, blowing a wisp of her blonde hair away from her face.

This happens every time I have an idea, Amanda thought. God, Joy can be so stubborn.

"What do we do? Sit here until the proof comes walking in the front door?"

Joy leaned back against the counter top of the employee kitchen between the Mr. Coffee and the sink.

"No, we don't wait for it to come walking in the door. Do you want to investigate? Then get to work with my blessings."

"Thank you."

"But think about this: If Mary Eileen did, just hypothetically, kill David Van Holt, what do you think she'll do to you or me if we get close to the truth?"

The thought did give Amanda pause. She knew Joy was right. They had come close before, very close to getting killed, when they tried to get the goods on a guy they suspected of being a serial killer.

We are amateurs, Amanda had to admit to herself.

"Okay. We are professional reporters, but we are not cops. We are not detectives," Amanda said, watching Joy nod affirmatively with every word that had become a mantra between the pair.

"So what do we do next?"

Amanda took a deep breath and prepared herself to say the words she hated.

"We go to the cops," she said.

"And?"

"We ask them what they have heard, tell them what we think, and go from there."

"Magnificent, my young protege," Joy said, reaching out to give Amanda's hand a short, furtive squeeze.

"Let's go talk to the cops," Amanda said.

"Let's go."

If they hadn't been at work, Amanda and Joy might have walked down the hall arm-in-arm. They were on another mission. Amanda couldn't have been happier. They were off on another quest for the truth. Joy couldn't have been more nervous.

On their way out of the kitchenette, they ran into Beatrice, the seventy-year-old matriarch of human resources. She was as much a fixture in the St. Isidore Chronicle as the pipes that rumbled under the building.

"Guess what now?" Beatrice said.

Amanda and Joy raised their eyebrows as if wondering why they should care about the answer to Beatrice's riddle. The answer was obvious. Now, Joy and Amanda were both wondering how to get out of this conversation as quickly as possible.

"David Van Holt just emailed his resignation. He quit. Just like that," she said with a snap of her fingers in the air.

"No kidding?" Joy looked at Amanda.

"Is he going to come in for his last check?"

"No need for that," Beatrice told Amanda. "We all get paid by direct deposit. His check will go out to the bank with all the others. Besides he said in his email that he had money saved and just got tired of working 9-to-5, Monday through Friday. Wrote something about going on an adventure."

"He just quit. No notice. No anything?" Joy said.

"And we'll never see him again," said Beatrice, as she walked down the hall, going back to her office to start the job search.

"And we'll never see him again," Amanda said.

"He quit."

"Isn't that convenient?"

ACROSS THE STREET, Mary Eileen leaned back in the chair at her dining room table and smiled. Now she was glad that David had always used her computer to do his freelance work at the Chronicle. His password couldn't have been easier to hack.

Eleven

Joy hadn't forgotten her apartment keys in a long time. But this morning she was so wiped out that she could forgive herself for this mistake.

The problem was that her car keys were on the same ring as her apartment keys so she'd have to see Russ, the apartment manager and ask his assistance.

Russ was an okay guy. Overweight, never able to tuck in his t-shirt — it was always some rock 'n roll shirt with a band from the 1970s or 80s screen printed on the front — and he was starting to do a combover on top, but Russ had turned out to be a decent human being.

A few years ago before Joy and Amanda made a name for themselves, he'd been a real prick to Joy. Russ seemed to relish the mornings when she'd have to ask him to let her into the apartment to retrieve her keys. But one morning when she was with Amanda, both of them delayed by her forgetfulness, Joy had seen the light — with Amanda's help.

"He's hot for you," Amanda said as Joy started her 2006 Kia Rio, bright red when it was new, dingy and dinged up now, but it was reliable, as long as the door locks didn't freeze in the winter.

"Oh, be real!"

"I am not kidding."

"He's a fucking jerk," Joy said as she blew the Kia's horn at one of the idiots who was driving too slow. Everybody slower than her was a moron. People who drove too fast were jackasses. That was Joy's rule of the road. The guy who was the recipient of her horn blast of the moment was not driving all that slow, but the horn made a nice punctuation point for Joy's frustration with Russ.

"You're right, he is. But he's only a jerk 'cuz he's trying too hard."

It turned out, Amanda was correct. Russ was still kind of a nerd, but wasn't Joy all about that? Believe it or not — oh God, Joy could sense Amanda's smirk if she admitted this — but Russ was a decent guy. He might even make an interesting remodeling challenging for a woman someday, Joy thought. Those t-shirts would be the first thing to go and forget the combover Russ; it doesn't fool anyone.

Of course, she hadn't gone that far, yet.

Russ smiled when Joy came into his office door. They hadn't seen each other for months. It had been a long time since she had forgotten her keys and Russ had run out of excuses to bump into her at the apartment complex. They had seen each other a couple of times at St. Isidore Gamer, the game shop downtown, and had spoken, but Russ wanted more.

So rather than acting the jerk — he'd been reading some self-improvement books that would be better categorized as 'wishful thinking' — Russ felt like he was ready when Joy walked into his office.

She didn't say a word. They both smiled and laughed as Russ got his master key set out, opened his office door for Joy and walked her back to her apartment.

The silence was comforting. Joy felt good walking beside Russ. It wasn't like they had any relationship besides that of tenant-apartment manager. Still, there was something about this guy, Joy thought, that was warm and cozy. And she liked warm and comfortable,

"Here you go," Russ said as he opened her door. He did it very gallantly, Joy thought. It had been eons since any man had treated her like this. It is the little things that count, right?

She hesitated for a moment, standing in the doorway, with Russ' arm stretched out, still holding the door knob. They were standing face to face, Joy breathing a bit heavier than she would have liked, as she licked her lower lip and said, "Coffee?"

Russ smiled and said, "Thank you." His encounter with Joy was going much better than he had imagined. Russ had wanted to talk to her for some time. There was something on his mind.

He'd never been comfortable with the girls in school or the women in the apartment complex. Russ had never been smooth with anyone, male or female, but he felt good with Joy. It wasn't a warm, cozy, comfortable feeling like it was when his mother came to visit. No, this was different. It was toastier than warm, nearly hot, as a matter of fact. For the first time in almost forever, Russ didn't feel like a fat boob.

They sat at the small, three-chair breakfast nook table in Joy's apartment and made small talk. Russ told her what it was like growing up in St. Isidore, she talked about her dreams, and he spoke of his.

But there was an awkward pause in the conversation. After the recitation of each other's resumes, it was time to talk about something more important; at least that's how Russ felt.

"I guess you're looking into David Van Holt, the guy who used to hang with that woman who runs the Coffee Shoppe," Russ said.

Joy had been hoping for more. She too had felt like the pause in their sentences should be the opening of a new chapter. You don't always get what you want, Joy realized.

She shifted into a semi-reporter mode, smiled, and waited for more.

"You know, he loved her, David did," Russ said speaking in a machine gun, rapid fire cadence that caught Joy's interest. She sat up straighter and touched Russ' hand. Joy sensed that Russ had something important to share.

"Everybody in town was laughing at David because he was refusing to leave Mary Eileen's apartment after their divorce. But, he couldn't leave. He had no one else. David loved her so much that he just thought if he hung on, if he toughed it out, she would fall back in love with him."

Joy squeezed Russ' hand. They were talking about love. She knew that Russ must want love as badly as David had desired Mary Eileen's affection. To want something so bad, Joy understood completely, yet never have a chance to win it, could burn a brand on your heart. She felt it almost every day.

"What do you think happened to him?"

Russ shrugged.

"He didn't just leave on his own, that's for sure. David would never leave Mary Eileen Sullivan. She was all he had."

Twelve

Neither Joy nor Amanda believed David had gone off on an adventure, at least not of his volition. It was all too convenient. First, the guy disappeared, then an email mysteriously appeared complete with his resignation and an explanation of his vanishing act.

"Come on, Chief Doolan, doesn't this make you just a little suspicious?" Joy said.

Lumpy Doolan felt like he was on another quick trip to nowhere. He'd been down this road before with these two reporters. Joy and Amanda had been sure one of St. Isidore High School's most beloved teachers was a serial killer. Doolan had given them one of his oldest detectives, who'd died for his trouble, and they had come up with nothing but a basement that might or might not have been a BDSM dungeon of death.

Joy and Amanda followed that up with a three-part shock series of articles about the Suicide Forest and all of the women who had wound up swinging from the trees for the past three decades or more. And then the crap they stirred up came tumbling downhill right into Chief Doolan's lap.

Now they expect me to get into bed with them again; Doolan thought and stewed at the sight of the two reporters on the other side of his desk.

"And what do we have to go on besides your suspicions?" Doolan said. "I mean is this going to be anything but shaking up a hornet's nest like you did last time? I got stung in the ass plenty over that fiasco."

"Fiasco?" an outraged Amanda yelled as she rose from her wooden chair in front of the Chief's desk.

"The only reason your investigation flopped was that you pulled back. The Chamber of Commerce started quaking in their boots about the Suicide Forest and what it would do to the town if there was a serial killer loose."

"Hold it right there, young lady," Doolan said as he pointed a fat index finger Amanda's way.

Joy put a hand on her ace reporter's wrist and not so gently led her back to her chair. The last thing they needed to do was to piss off Doolan again. It was bad enough they had to remind him of the shit storm that rained on his parade the last time they had all gotten together.

"Oh, no," Amanda said, refusing to sit down even though Joy's grip on her wrist was tightening.

"Oh, no, nobody wanted to admit a serial killer was targeting young girls, women and even some boys and men. Oh no, it was so much easier to make believe that all of these people, especially the teenage girls, had been killing themselves."

"You need to sit down," Doolan said as he rose from his chair, a troubling sign, and Joy knew it. Any time Doolan got his 300-plus pounds of muscle encased in fat moving there was going to be a conflict. The man did not waste energy.

"Okay hold on, everyone," Joy said as she rose to the rescue of her young protege.

"Chief, nobody is saying you or anyone in your department shirked their duty or anything like that. But what we are saying is whatever happened in the Tim Sheldon investigation is history. This is new. Let's move forward."

Doolan would have loved to have tossed these women out of his office. Hell, he'd like to have thrown them out his sixth-floor window. But the Shapiro family that had been publishing the St. Isidore Chronicle for years had too much weight in this town. If there was one thing

Doolan had grown adept at over his past thirty years in office, it was dodging storms that rained down hail shaped like turds.

"Okay, granted this is new. But where is the evidence that anything is wrong here? The guy, this David what's-his-name, sent an email explaining he was resigning and going off on some weird quest. He's a millennial for Christ's sake. That's what they do."

"He was in love with Mary Eileen."

"And you think she killed him."

"Could have, that's all I am saying, Chief Doolan," Amanda said.

"And if there is a 'could have killed' in this case, why not help us investigate?" Joy said.

"Why would she kill him?"

"They were divorced," Joy said.

"So, what? Lots of people get divorced. Most of them don't wind up dead. Hell, if more marriages split up quicker the murder rate would probably be a lot lower."

"Everybody in town knows David was refusing to leave Mary Eileen's apartment," said Amanda.

"And he got killed for that? Because he was, I don't know, what? Eating her food?"

"She was having an affair with Hans Mueller," said Joy. "They are still together."

"Again, 'so what?'" Doolan said. "Half of the people in this town are sleeping with the other half."

"They don't all have guns," said Amanda.

"Mary Eileen Sullivan has a gun?" Doolan asked.

"And she is trained to shoot to kill," said Amanda.

Doolan eased back in his tilt chair, looking at the suspended ceiling. Amanda held her breath. Joy counted the seconds clicking by on the wall clock.

Chief Doolan leaned forward as slowly as any large, powerful man would who knows he doesn't need to move quickly for a couple of female reporters.

"Ladies, think about this from my point of view, the point of view of a professional," Doolan said in his most condescending, authoritarian voice.

"You have a motive; I will give you that. I can believe that Mary Eileen might have wanted David what's-his-name dead. Okay. Means? You say she knew how to shoot and had a gun. Granted. So there's motive and means. Opportunity? Well, yeah. They lived together, whether they wanted it or not."

"That's just what I have been saying since Day One," Amanda said raising her fist in victory as she jumped out of her chair.

"But what we are still missing something," the Chief said in a stage whisper building tension and easing Amanda off her victorious cloud-nine.

Amanda and Joy were on the edges of their chairs.

"We don't have a body," Doolan roared. "Bring me a body, and we have a murder. But don't get me a body and as far as I am concerned, nobody got killed."

Amanda and Joy shrunk in their chairs.

"Now ladies, that's the door," Doolan said, pointing over their heads.

"Please don't let it hit you where the Lord split you."

As soon as Joy and Amanda left, Doolan reached for his buzzing smartphone. State Police Commander Jack Hart was calling.

Thirteen

After the murder of David Van Holt, Mary Eileen and Hans Mueller tried to keep their May-December relationship a secret. However, they could only keep it quiet so long in a town like St. Isidore.

Not long after she cut up David's body, encased its pieces and parts in cement, and planted him in the cellar, but not so soon that the neighbors became suspicious, Hans moved in with Mary Eileen.

"Unsere Liebe wird ewig dauern," Hans said to her as they lay in bed, their bed, for the first time.

"What does that mean?"

"Say it after me."

"No, what does it mean?"

He put his fingertip on Mary Eileen's lips. She laughed as she pulled back and bit Hans' finger.

He laughed.

"Unsere."

"Unsere"

"Liebe"

"Liebe"

"wird"

"wird"

"Ewig dauern"

"Ewig dauern."

Mary Eileen looked at Hans and raised her eyebrows as if to ask, "What's next?"

"That means, 'our love will last forever,'" Hans said.

"Our love will last forever," she repeated, "unsere Liebe wird ewig dauern."

Hans laughed at her clumsy attempt at German. But Mary Eileen didn't care.

She was as happy as a teenager in love. Mary Eileen had fallen under this older man's spell. He wasn't all that much her senior, only a decade. But still, those ten years made a lot of difference to both of these not-so-young lovers.

For one, it meant he finally had a woman who would be truly submissive to him. Or at least, that is what Hans believed.

As for Mary Eileen, the age difference gave more credence to what she wanted to believe — that she had finally found a father figure who would make her happy and be completely devoted to showing her a more comfortable life.

Why shouldn't she be pleased?

Not only had she found a man to love, Mary Eileen finally had someone to share her life.

And their days together started out as a good life. St. Isidore County was filled with small thumb lakes. Hans had a cottage on one of them, and Mary Eileen was amazed to find out, he also had a boat.

The cottage was right on the lake. It was actually waterfront property that was isolated enough that Han and Mary Eileen could make love in the cabin, in the woods or even on the sand of the beach at night without anyone seeing or hearing them.

St. Isidore might have been a minor league city that screamed average, but the town did have a couple of community theaters, music halls, and even some top-name talent would perform at the Van Andel Arena on Sundays as a stop between the real cities.

There was also the Suicide Forest. Mary Eileen had driven by it, but never had the courage to go inside even though she'd been totally up close and personal with the murder and disposal of one, David Van Holt.

Hans was afraid of nothing. Together, they spent a night in the Forest, part of a guided tour that included actors playing the parts of some of the famous people who had died in the Forest.

Hans had even found two new dead bodies that earned him a slot on the St. Isidore Famous Deadies List, the people who had discovered fresh corpses in the Forest.

Looking around the Forest, Mary Eileen wished she had been able to get David's fat-ass body into the trunk of her car. She would have loved to have dropped him off under one of these giant trees.

Hans wanted Mary Eileen to tell him all of her wishes so he could make them come true. She was not shy, as evidenced by a strand of real pearls around her neck, the largest diamond ring she found in a downtown jewelry store, and a new car.

Transporting David to the Forest was the only wish she wouldn't share. Why ruin a good thing, right?

Mary Eileen Sullivan was happy.

It didn't last.

There was a huge void in her life. Mary Eileen wasn't sad. She just was not truly satisfied, not yet. She needed more than Hans could provide. And the truth was, Mary Eileen Sullivan did not trust Hans Mueller.

She soon realized Hans was not her Prince Charming and never would be. He was as controlling as David had been. In a way, it was worse. Because he was ten years older than Mary Eileen, she was even more in his power. Or at least he thought she was.

She felt trapped, imprisoned like she was going through life with a plastic bag over her head.

And what was worse was that Mary Eileen felt like — no, she knew — Hans was cheating on her. Hans didn't make a secret of his dalliances. To him, it was just part of being a man, a real man. If Mary Eileen knows, so what, Hans thought. What's she going to do about it?

If only David were there; he could have answered the question for Hans.

Of course, Hans had no idea what was about to happen, but as far as Mary Eileen was concerned, his fate was sealed.

He'd be her second kill.

But this time, it would be easier.

Mary Eileen had learned that shooting someone to death was relatively straightforward. The hard part was getting rid of the evidence, the largest piece of which was the body.

Looking back at her experience with David, Mary Eileen decided she needed to get better at using the chainsaw that was still in the cellar and mixing concrete, which also was waiting for her in what had become Hans' final resting place.

She needed to go to a professional. No, not a hit man.

Mary Eileen went back to the stores where she had purchased the saw and the concrete and signed up for the advanced courses the retailers had for their professional construction customers.

When she was ready, this time, Mary Eileen was really ready.

She was prepared to confront Hans.

Fourteen

Hans and Mary Eileen were drinking whiskey after an evening out with friends before they got into a drunken argument. They had thrown off their clothes with the abandon of teenage lovers whose parents were away for the night and raced to the bed.

All went well, until Hans made a mistake.

"What did you say?" Mary Eileen said with just a hint of slurred words and way more Irish brogue than was normal. She'd had more than her share of Jameson's out of a bottle Hans had brought home from the restaurant. Mixing it with wine had sharpened her wits, or so she thought.

Hans put his arms around her and squeezed as he picked her up off the bed.

"What did you call me," she said.

Hans held her a little tighter, tensing — Mary Eileen could feel the muscles in his arms tighten up. He was behind her. She could feel him getting hard and then softening against her butt.

"I asked," Hans said, "if you had a good time tonight with Cathy and Phil."

"No, you didn't, you fucking pig," Mary Eileen said as she spun around to face him and push his arms down and his body away from her.

"You called me, 'Cathy,'" Mary Eileen said. "You drifted off in your mind. You were pretending you were with her."

Cathy was even younger that Mary Eileen. She was much cuter and even spoke German, as least enough to get Hans to laugh at a couple of jokes that neither Phil nor Mary Eileen could understand at dinner.

"I did not," Hans said. He stood straight up. His six-foot-four-inch frame towered over Mary Eileen by nearly a foot. It was usually enough to scare her into submission. Some nights she liked that. In the beginning, she had loved it. He was so much like her father, Michael, as she remembered him in the Old Country.

But it wasn't working for either of them, tonight.

"You fucking are hot for her," Mary Eileen said, bouncing a fingertip off his chest.

Hans had opened his shirt at dinner, pretending it was too warm. God, how I hate that, Mary Eileen had thought at the time.

It wasn't the wine or the Jameson's that had her simmering. She had simmered at dinner. Mary Eileen was close to a full boil, now.

"You always have been," she continued. "Every fucking woman you fucking see, you have to think about fucking them."

"I do not. You need to calm down, young lady."

"Young lady? Who the fuck do you think you are talking to?"

"I'm talking to a fucking brat, that's who I'm talking to," Hans said. "See, I can drop the F-bomb too."

Hans took a step toward her.

She took a step back.

He reached toward her and ran his fingers through her thick, auburn hair which had fallen to her shoulders after the red ribbon that had been holding it disappeared.

Mary Eileen took another step back and grabbed Hans' hand to keep it away from her hair

"Sie sind mein schönes Mädchen," Hans said, "ich werde dich immer lieben."

Mary Eileen stopped. Now she held Hans by the wrist and moved a step closer to him.

My beautiful girl, I will love you always, Mary Eileen translated to herself. Hans had taught her a few phrases in German, phrases he wanted her to know. She might not have gotten every word correct, but she understood.

Even though Mary Eileen didn't think she could trust Hans to keep his big thing out of any girl or woman who offered, she gave in. His blue eyes, cold silver hair, wide shoulders and that goddamn dimple on the left side of his face always does it, she thought.

She stepped closer to him.

Hans put both arms around her waist and drew Mary Eileen tight against his chest. She could feel his heat beating.

"Und ich bin dein, Daddy," she said, "und ich bin dein. I am yours, Daddy."

It was time for some intense role play. She could feel how excited Hans had become and that aroused Mary Eileen.

They went to bed and made love as a father and his little girl.

But this was not settled as far as Mary Eileen was concerned. Even while she was making love to Hans, she was thinking about how to get even with him and best-case scenario; be free of him

When she returned from the bathroom, Mary Eileen sat on her side of the bed, placed her hand on Hans' chest, and told him that she still loved him and always would.

Hans rolled over on his side, facing away from her and went to sleep. To add insult to injury, he began snoring.

Hans was ignoring her. She might have been able to tolerate that, but he was also snoring. That was the final straw.

Mary Eileen was enraged.

The Beretta was under the mattress on her side of the bed.

While Hans rested peacefully, snoring perhaps as gently as a man could, Mary Eileen reached under the bed. Her hand came back with the pistol, the same gun she had used to kill David.

Hans was on his side, facing away from Mary Eileen. He was still snoring. If he hadn't been snoring, Mary Eileen might have stopped. But he didn't, so she didn't. Holding her breath, she pressed the barrel the gun against the back his head and fired. The first one was the tough one. After that, Mary Eileen squeezed off four more shots into the back of her lover's head.

Each .22 caliber bullet made a relatively clean entrance. Like with David, most of the bullets stayed inside his skull, ricocheting through Han's brain, chewing up tissue and his life as they went. But those that exited Han's head blew a decent-sized hole in his face.

The bed was a mess. It was worse than the brains, blood, skull fragments and God knows what else coated the dining room table after David's execution. His remains had fallen on a wooden table and a tile floor.

Hans' remains soaked deep into the mattress.

Mary Eileen was breathing fast and furiously. Her heart was racing. Once her breathing slowed, she crept to the bedroom window and sighed as quietly as possible, trying to sense if the neighbors had heard anything.

The night was still. Everything was quiet. Mary Eileen calmed herself, walked into the living room, laid down on the couch, and went to sleep. She knew from the last time; there was no need to rush.

THE NEXT MORNING SHE went back into the bedroom, where Hans' body was still lying on the bed. Even more so than she had been with David's corpse, Mary Eileen was racked with guilt.

Mary Eileen knelt beside the bed, touched his hand and asked Hans for his forgiveness before she began the process of disposing of his body.

It was early Sunday morning. The neighborhood was as quiet as it had been several hours ago when Mary Eileen first squeezed the trigger on the Beretta. Beyond the task that lay ahead of her, she had no worries.

Mary Eileen knew it was time to go to work. She dragged Hans' body downstairs to the cellar where the chainsaw and cement were waiting.

"I guess Cheryl is going to hear the coffee grinder again," Mary Eileen said to herself.

Fifteen

When Sean Patrick Flynn walked into the Coffee Shoppe it wasn't a case of love at first sight — well, there was some of that — but it was most certainly lust at first glance, at least for Mary Eileen.

He walked in with none of the false bravado of Hans. He didn't have the German's swagger or the attitude of the guy who had always been the biggest, strongest kid on the playground. Sean didn't have the faux intellectualism of David. And there was certainly none of David's mama's boy attitude about Sean.

Mary Eileen sensed it immediately, the way a dog might sense another canine that he or she both wants and needs. Yeah, there was a strong scent of animal magnetism at play.

Mary Eileen could tell immediately the man who had walked into the Coffee Shoppe, this man for whom the rest of humanity parted just as the Red Sea did for Moses was special. And he felt it so strongly he didn't have to tell anyone else.

Here was a man who never whined, a man who never pushed or bullied, who was supremely confident enough to make others the center of attention.

And then, he spoke.

"Good morning," the man said with a smile. His warm, blue eyes met Mary Eileen's green eyes. He didn't drill into her soul or anything like that. It was more of a soft touch, a caressing of everything that was Mary Eileen.

He didn't take her breath away. Instead, he made it easy for her to speak.

"Good morning, to you," Mary Eileen answered. "I'm Mary Eileen Sullivan. And I am here to serve you. What'll you have today?"

Her Irish brogue was a bit more pronounced than usual, but it rolled off her tongue so easily. And the best part was, it matched his to perfection.

Mary Eileen Sullivan felt that she was home again.

"And my name is Sean Patrick Flynn, Ms. Mary Eileen Sullivan. I am very pleased to meet you," he said, " and I will have one of your tall, dark coffees."

A "thank you" and a "you're welcome, come again," later, this conversation was finished. That was all. But it was enough for Mary Eileen.

The first time Mary Eileen spoke with Sean might have been only a short customer-barista kind of conversation. But it left her with the feeling that she was the most important, unique person with whom he had spoken that day. Nothing else mattered more at the moment he ordered a tall, dark coffee than Mary Eileen. At least that's the way he made her feel.

"Tall and dark he is not, but he is perfect for you, no?" Christina whispered as Sean left the Coffee Shoppe. "He was just like a white Denzel Washington, the way he looked at you and talked to you."

The next time, Sean and Mary Eileen spoke a few more words and they exchanged a few more words during the transaction after that. Eventually, the counter between them would disappear. But Sean was showing Mary Eileen the courtesy of taking his time as if he had all the time in the world for something that was good enough to last the rest of their lives.

Sean came into the Coffee Shoppe a fourth time, about a week after his first coffee, and invited Mary Eileen to join him at one of the round, wooden tables by the window.

She glanced back at Christina, received a nod and a wink signifying she could handle the two or three customers in line, and said, "Of course, I would love too."

They talked for an hour. Mary Eileen and Sean discovered their ancestors had lived near each other in Ireland.

They both loved football, or soccer as the heathens in America would call the game, even though they rooted for opposing teams. The sports debate that followed added a vibrant, nearly erotic, flashpoint to their relationship even before they had undressed each other for the first time.

Christina refilled coffees with the grace of a Five-Star restaurant hostess, never intruding, but never far away in case she was needed.

Mary Eileen told Sean more about herself than she had told anyone, even Christina.

She spoke of her life in Dublin, why she left Ireland, landing in New York, and how she came to be in St. Isidore.

She told him about everything and everyone except David and Hans.

Sean spoke with what the Americans in the Coffee Shoppe would consider to be a soft Irish brogue, an accent that Mary Eileen didn't hear. To her, he was speaking as everyone spoke, or at least as she spoke, with a smile never leaving his face. He too talked about how he came to America, much like Mary Eileen did, and how he had decided to stay in America.

"He's a visiting professor of literature, from Dublin," Christina told several customers the next day. "His name is Sean Patrick Flynn. He works at the University of Michigan, but he should be on TV. Isn't he just perfect?"

Their initial conversation would be only the first time they shared stories and life experiences. That was the best phrase to describe what Mary Eileen and Sean did. They shared.

Their relationship was not as fast, furious, or frenzied, as that of two teenagers in the backseat of Daddy's car. Mary Eileen was not racing to the finish line because she couldn't stand to spend even one more night alone. Neither was Sean. They were not looking for a one-night stand. They were seeking something more.

An author in her bed, and an Irish author at that. Mary Eileen was thrilled.

She certainly didn't feel like a woman in her thirties who'd lived through two terrible love affairs that had ended tragically.

No, Mary Eileen felt like she had begun a renaissance, a new life, with someone who was not only incredibly attractive and a beautiful lover; but a person who could quickly become her best —and only — friend.

Seventeen

Christina told her that she "looked radiant" when she walked into the Coffee Shoppe, and that is just how Mary Eileen felt. Again this morning, she'd awakened with Sean in her bed. They'd had breakfast together, showered together, and made love — just a quickie — before he bounded down the stairs and she waved goodbye as he hopped on his motorcycle and rode away.

They'd been a couple for three months, and it seemed to get better every day. But this day was exceptional.

The night before Mary Eileen had pressed Sean about the book he was writing.

"You're doing something that millions of people dream about, Sean. You are writing a book."

"It's not that big of a deal," Sean replied, his Irish brogue a little heavier than usual. He was feeling sleepy, but doing his best to stay awake by concentrating on the luxurious sheet wrapped around his naked body. "You must spend a fortune on these sheets," Sean had mentioned after their third night together. She'd laughed and led him by the hand down the hall to her linen closet. Mary Eileen opened the door as if she were showing off the wizard behind the curtain. Comforters, pillowcases, sheets, shams and more filled the linen cabinet "no less than $500 per set," she proudly proclaimed.

"Of course, it's a big deal," Mary Eileen said, returning Sean's attention to the matter at hand, which was her need to know more about what he was doing.

"It's not the kind of thing most people will read."

"Why not?"

"It's not a murder mystery or a Harry Potter knock-off; it's about literature. It's to be a book about books."

"Intelligent people will read it. I will read it."

"Oh, I am sure you will, my love. You will be one of the few, just as you are one of the few who understands Sean Patrick Flynn."

"So tell me more. What are you going to write? What kind of literature?"

"The literature of life and love, death and guilt."

Mary Eileen, despite herself, pulled back from her lover. Not far, but she certainly flinched.

Sean looked at her with questioning eyes and a slight, wry smile. He lifted an eyebrow.

"Are you all right, my pet? You looked quite pale for a moment."

"What do you mean?" Mary Eileen responded quickly, perhaps too quickly.

"You looked shocked and like you might be ill."

"No, I am fine. Tell me more."

Sean paused and caught his breath. He had trouble focusing on such an erudite explanation while holding Mary Eileen's nude body. Her hand running up and down his thigh didn't help his concentration.

But as any good professor would, Sean prepared himself to address his class.

"From Dante's Inferno to Crime and Punishment by Dostoevsky, and in modern times, Portnoy's Complaint, the great authors and minds have written about life and love, death, and guilt."

"What did they say?"

"I believe they have all described the relationship between life, love, death and guilt as a guiding force that shapes who we are and who we become," Sean said.

Mary Eileen didn't pull back, but her eyes told Sean she was drifting away.

He touched her bare shoulder.

"Think about us, Mary Eileen Sullivan. We are both Irish Catholic. 'Our guilt becomes our shame, our lacerating shame,' Edna O'Brien wrote. 'When anyone asks me about the Irish character, I say look at the trees. Maimed, stark and misshapen, but ferociously tenacious.'"

Mary Eileen was stunned. It was like Sean had slapped her across the face, not in a vicious way, or even a punishing way. It was more like an emotional alarm clock was ringing in her ears.

"Have you never felt guilt?" Sean whispered. "Is there anything you are afraid to tell me?"

Mary Eileen didn't respond. She had heard, but she was not listening.

"Maimed, stark and misshapen, but ferociously tenacious," Mary Eileen muttered, not quite a whisper, but Sean still had to strain to listen.

She gripped his hand, and he hers.

"I have felt guilty. Haven't we all?"

"Of course we have," Sean said.

They waited. Each expecting, hoping, the other would speak next. Finally, Sean began.

"I left the scene of a traffic accident, once," Sean said after taking a deep breath.

"That's not so terrible," Mary Eileen said with a little laugh. "What was it; a fender bender in a parking lot?"

Sean paused again to gather himself. Mary Eileen looked up expectantly and saw Sean close his eyes.

"No, it was not in a parking lot," he said in a whisper. "I was driving late one night from Dublin to Belfast."

"Along the Irish Sea? I remember those roads."

"I had been drinking. A woman was with me. Another car was coming at us; I swerved, the other car left the road and hit a tree," Sean said. "We stopped, I stopped, I could have gotten out to make sure the people in that other vehicle were all right. But I didn't."

Mary Eileen felt the muscles of his forearm twitch as she tightened his grip she hoped reassuringly.

"I didn't get out," Sean continued. "We drove off. Next morning, listening to the BBC, we found out they were dead; the two people in the car that hit the tree."

"Oh my God," Mary Eileen said. "But they might have been killed instantly. There was probably nothing you could have done."

"But what if they were not dead? What if I could have gotten them some help? It is guilt that I live with," Sean said. "Do you hate me now?"

Mary Eileen's gaze never wavered from his eyes. She said, "There is nothing you should be afraid to tell me, Sean, my love. Your heart is an open book to me. I have bared my body, my heart and my soul without fear, without shame. You should feel that you can do the same, always."

She snuggled against him as Sean put his strong arm around her breasts and held her tight, her back feeling fresh and comfortable against his chest.

They fell asleep like that, each reassured by the others' proximity and nudity. Sean and Mary Eileen were a couple, closer than either had ever been to another.

A quick, strong breeze from the open window across the room and the sound of fluttering and flapping curtains roused Sean. He blinked, rubbed his eyes, and ever so gently slid out from underneath Mary Eileen. While he flexed his fingers and moved his arm to ease the tingle from the blood flowing again, he watched Mary Eileen's breasts rise and fall slowing and softly as she slept. He had not awakened her. She was peaceful, as she should be, Sean thought.

As slowly and gently as he had slid out from under Mary Eileen, Sean eased out of bed, barely lifting the comforter and white sheet for fear of waking his love.

He took his smartphone off the night table and padded carefully out of the bedroom, down the hall, over the brown, bamboo wooden floor, slowly turned the door knob of the bathroom, flicked on the light and touched the home key of his phone.

While he waited the millisecond it would take to open the smartphone app he needed; Sean opened the medicine cabinet over the sink. Paxil, Prozac, and other drugs he recognized as SNRI's and SSRI's for treating anxiety and depression filled the cabinet.

Seeing the message app had opened, Sean gently closed the medicine cabinet and returned his attention to the smartphone.

Sean scrolled through the messages before finding the "?" message he had received a few days ago.

"Closer," he texted.

Eighteen

"Mary Eileen Sullivan, look at you," she said to her reflection in the bathroom mirror. Her skin was radiant. Her eyes glowed and sparkled.

Mary Eileen had never felt this good. Of all the men in her life, Sean Patrick Flynn was the exception.

And now their relationship was taking another step forward. Mary Eileen and Sean were going on a trip together, a vacation, back to their homeland, Ireland. And most importantly, they were going as a couple.

"We leave out of Detroit Metro at 8:15 am Friday," Sean had told her the night before.

It was all so spontaneous. That made it even better.

Mary Eileen was so excited the night after Sean told her of their vacation she stayed up until nearly 3 a.m. packing. She had a couple of days before she would catch the flight with Sean, but why wait?

The next morning her excitement grew to a point where she landed on a plateau of complete happiness. Mary Eileen could feel Sean's hands on her back even though he was hundreds of miles away. His aroma was everywhere in her little apartment.

The sun was up and shining through her kitchen window. She was doing the breakfast dishes when a cloud passed over the sun, and her kitchen went dark for a sliver of a second.

It happened so quickly that Mary Eileen caught her breath. Was it going to storm?

She caught her breath as the water suddenly stopped flowing through the kitchen faucet. Then a second later it started again.

She never thought of herself as being a superstitious woman, but Mary Eileen had to wonder aloud, "What does this all mean?"

Her smartphone buzzed on the tile counter to her left. She quickly dried her hands while looking at the name on the phone to see who was calling before she picked it up.

"Shit," she said to herself.

It was Christina. Something was wrong at the Coffee Shoppe.

Her right hand moved toward the phone and then stopped.

"Why would I want to come down from this high?" Mary Eileen said to herself.

It was probably nothing. Just a late delivery or a problem with one of the machines. Whatever the snafu was, it all seemed so trivial now.

Mary Eileen would deal with it later.

First, she wanted a shower. She wanted to be naked with the water running over her, pretending her hands were Sean's hands. The Coffee Shoppe could wait. It was going to be a good day for Christina, too. Mary Eileen was going to tell her about the vacation, tell her she was going to be in charge, and the best part was that Christina was going to get the business. They had already signed the papers. If everything went as Mary Eileen expected, she would never return to little St. Isidore. There was no reason she and Sean couldn't build a life together in Ireland.

Meanwhile, downstairs, Christina was panicking. Customers stood in three lines, four deep, at the counter as the employees looked at each other with shrugged shoulders and raised eyebrows.

What could they do? There was no water. Christina had heard what sounded like water rushing in the cellar below. She had run downstairs only to find the water had stopped completely.

Over the sound of a dozen different conversations, customers and employees heard the unmistakable sound of Christina running up the rickety wooden steps.

She ran into the Coffee Shoppe, skidding on wet shoes over the polished hardwood floor. When Christina slid to a stop, she grabbed her smartphone and pounded out a text message to Mary Eileen.

One word: FLOOD!

Mary Eileen heard the chime tone on her phone signaling a text message from Christina had come in, just as she stood naked outside her shower stall turning the faucet handles back and forth wondering what was wrong with the water.

She was only a few moments away from being knocked off her plateau of happiness.

Now, Mary Eileen grabbed her phone and saw Christina's text. A cold shudder moved through her body, and she immediately started sweating.

Mary Eileen had felt a little nauseous earlier. Now she was ready to vomit. And she did but choked it back and swallowed hard.

"Plumbers?" She texted to Christina.

"On the way," Christina replied.

Mary Eileen had to sit down. She flipped the lid down and sat on the toilet, weighing her options.

Sean was waiting for her, or soon would be, at Detroit Metro Airport. If the plumbers found the body parts of David and Hans in the cellar, she would run. But until they found something, there was no reason to change her plans, Mary Eileen decided.

It would be better to be cool, calm, and collected.

"Let's go downstairs and see what is going on," she said to herself. Mary Eileen was confident that even though this was a stressful situation she had pushed the big chunks of concrete containing the parts and pieces of her ex and her former far enough back so that they could not be seen.

Mary Eileen didn't want to raise any suspicions by running off like a mad woman. After all, Joy and Amanda already thought she had killed

David. They hadn't asked about Hans yet, but that was only a matter of time.

However, if the plumbers did find something, Mary Eileen wanted to be ready.

Just in case, she packed an extra bag and put both suitcases by the front door, so she could just reach in and grab them on the fly.

If worst came to worst, Mary Eileen knew she had to run. Then she would have to reinvent herself all over again.

But there was no need to do either until she knew for sure.

Nineteen

Mary Eileen was nervous. She was scared. On the inside, she was falling apart. But outwardly, no one would have been able to detect the slightest tremor. But Mary Eileen was deathly afraid the plumbers below would find death in the cellar under the Coffee Shoppe.

Her worst fears were realized when she heard first one man and then another cry out.

Their screams echoed from under her feet. The sound of their voices bounced and slammed from rock wall to concrete ceiling and then come roaring out of the cellar door.

The men below were panicked. Working in proximity to all manner of sewers, sludge, and human waste as they did daily, these plumbers thought they had seen it all. With their discovery today, they had.

The men had frozen in place when the beams of their flashlights had spotted the first rock, if that is what it was, a cement stone with a human's leg sticking out. And then there was another, this time they got closer and found a hand sticking out of a hunk of cement. The last and final rock with the back of a human head visible is what did it.

Their cell phones wouldn't work in the cellar. They had to run upstairs, nearly knocking down a couple of Coffee Shoppe customers to get outside where they could breathe fresh air before vomiting on the sidewalk.

None of the customers knew what the plumbers had seen.

Mary Eileen knew what they had found. She hadn't done a good enough job covering the body parts with cement.

She also knew what had to happen next. She tapped the ride-sharing app on her smartphone. She was ready to go.

Mary Eileen walked quickly back upstairs, avoiding contact with the customers who were still reeling from the fleeing plumbers. Mary Eileen marched. She didn't run. Mary Eileen did not want to set off any alarms of suspicion before she had too. But still she didn't hesitate to shove a couple of people out of her way.

What would St. Isidore think of Mary Eileen Sullivan? She couldn't have cared less. Mary Eileen knew she was leaving the Coffee Shoppe for the last time. She would never return. Besides a couple of bags already packed, Mary Eileen was leaving her life behind. She would have to start all over again.

The rest of her belongings, her business, her obligations to creditors, her responsibilities to her employees, her life, especially the body parts of her ex-husband and ex-lover — it would all be erased from her life.

Mary Eileen was no longer scared or even nervous. She was on total autopilot. Her adrenaline was running high and fast, but it was completely under control. She felt just a little nauseous, but no less confident than when she'd left New York after dealing with a chef who had nearly raped her in a freezer.

Long story told short; she'd left him for dead with an ice pick in his chest.

Just as then, Mary Eileen had no doubt she could handle what came next. She was supremely confident of her ability to reinvent herself.

All she had to do was to get out of St. Isidore as quickly and smoothly as possible.

Where to go next? That question did give Mary Eileen a reason to pause. When the Uber driver showed up in the alley behind the Coffee Shoppe she took time to think about her next move, but only for a moment.

Mary Eileen made a decision. One word said it all.

"Drive," she said.

MARY EILEEN TOLD THE driver to go north from lower Michigan to the state's Upper Peninsula. She left the cityscape of St. Isidore behind, drove through a relatively flat landscape of farms, and then rows of magnificent evergreen and pine trees.

The ride was beautiful. With the shockingly blue panorama of Lake Michigan outside the window on her left, Mary Eileen was traveling through the most magnificent scenery Michigan had to offer. But she didn't see the lake. She didn't see the forests. She only saw herself losing Sean Patrick Flynn.

That hurt more than anything. Mary Eileen knew it was only a matter of time before the police put together the evidence and concluded that she had killed David and Hans. After that, they would not have to waste any time searching for her. Mary Eileen knew better than anyone that a person couldn't just vanish in this day and age of GPS and smartphones that showed the NSA where you lived. Even if somebody had been shot in the head, drawn and quartered and buried in cement; they would be discovered. It was only a matter of time before the police found her.

And she knew that as soon as he was told what had happened, Sean would decide that he was done with her.

God, that hurt Mary Eileen. She had finally found her true love. She had just found him too late. And there would be no way to win him back.

Mary Eileen sighed. What was done, was done. She would have to start anew.

Even the day after she'd dealt with the chef in New York wasn't the first time Mary Eileen had to reinvent herself.

She knew this time would not be the last, not unless she found another man just like Sean. But Mary Eileen had no misconceptions about the likelihood of that.

As soon as the Uber driver crossed the Mackinac Bridge into the Upper Peninsula, Mary Eileen told him to turn around and drive back down the Lower Peninsula to the Detroit area. She had to go to Ann Arbor, the University of Michigan. She might reinvent herself, but Mary Eileen would not surrender. Sean was her one true love. There would never be another. She had to find him. She had to win him back.

But first, Mary Eileen had to get away from the cops in St. Isidore. She knew they'd be after her and probably the state police, too. She would search for Sean. She would find Sean. However, that would have to wait. First, Mary Eileen Sullivan had to find shelter so that she could reinvent herself.

Mary Eileen needed to find another man.

Twenty

"What do you mean, she's gone?" Chief Lumpy Doolan said.

"I mean she's gone. She's not there. There is no sign of her. How many ways can I say it? There is no one in her apartment. She is not in the Coffee Shoppe. Mary Eileen Sullivan has vanished," the most obnoxious man in the room, as far as Doolan was concerned, State Police Detective Sean Patrick Flynn replied.

"But she was just here."

"And now she's not."

Fantastic, just fucking incredible, Doolan thought to himself. Murders just didn't happen in St. Isidore. Well, no, that wasn't entirely correct. The truth is that homicides happened all the time in the city that was wrapped around the world-famous Suicide Forest. But they were always classified as "suicides" or maybe "accidental deaths." The victims, if that is what the corpses could be called, almost always wound up hanging from a rope in the Forest, or laying on the ground, propped up next to one of the majestic trees upon which the world was drawn to die.

Doolan had told the state police there was nothing to the St. Isidore Chronicle story about some guy named David who had disappeared and might have been murdered. The reporters had received emails after the story came out explaining that he had just split town, needed a vacation, something like that. "After all," Doolan had argued, "if he wasn't alive and well, who could have been sending out the emails. The guy must have had a password, right?"

However, there was no sense trying the to tell the state cops anything, and once they sent this kid Sean Patrick Flynn to town undercover, Doolan knew it was going to be a shitty month.

Then another somebody that nobody in St. Isidore could ever even remember seeing vanished, or at least that's what the Chronicle's two superstar reporters had written, Doolan thought sarcastically.

That really sent Sean Patrick Flynn and his state police bosses into an uproar.

Doolan told them nothing was going on. People came and went all the time in St. Isidore. "Okay, we can search the Forest," Doolan had conceded. That was SOP anyway. Whenever his department got a missing person report, no matter how looney, the first thing they did was search the trees of the Suicide Forest. They didn't always find the missing person the first time, but leave it to the Deadie tourist brigade, the people who spent their vacation time searching for corpses in the Forest, and eventually, they would find the body.

Doolan figured that was a good plan this time too when this guy named Hans turned up missing. But, oh no, thanks to the Chronicle the state police sent an undercover cop, this Sean Patrick Flynn to town, to try to pin the killings on one of Doolan's favorite St. Isidorians, Mary Eileen Sullivan.

Okay. Fine. Doolan was willing to admit he might have been wrong about David and Hans, but for the love of God why did the parts and pieces have to be found in the basement under Mary Eileen Sullivan's coffee shop.

Still, Doolan thought, what does this prove?

"There's a chainsaw down there, and a couple of open bags of cement mix," said Sean, hands on hips, totally in his element, finally, he figured, getting some respect.

"Oh fuck," Doolan muttered under his breath.

"Yeah, and there's more," Sean said.

Doolan put his fat face into his hands and waited.

"We used the ultra-violet light and found blood splatters all over the cellar," Sean said. "Of course we expected that."

"So, what did you find that you didn't expect?"

Sean had no trouble hearing what the chief had asked, but because he wanted to see Doolan's face, he said, "Pardon me?"

Slowly the police chief raised his face from his hands. Sean saw the look of a fighter in Doolan's eyes, the look of an ugly man who suddenly had nothing left to lose. And Sean reminded himself that while Doolan had put on seventy-five pounds since his fighting days, this guy had been the heavyweight boxing champ of the U. S. Navy in his prime.

Sean backed off the accelerator of sarcasm just a bit when he replied, "We found blood stains going up the stairs, right to the door of Mary Eileen's apartment."

"You didn't go inside?"

"We need a warrant."

"I thought you had a key."

"BODY PARTS IN CEMENT, who'd a' thought?" Amanda said with a typical millennial smirk lighting her face.

"You'd a' thought," Joy said. God, she hated it when Amanda played cute. Well, just as Chief Doolan told himself the lie about murders in St. Isidore, Joy knew that she loved it when Amanda played cute and coy. Just not now, when they had potentially the biggest story the St. Isidore Chronicle had ever covered.

Body parts of one man, maybe two, found encased in cement stuffed in the back of an old stone cellar under downtown St. Isidore. The whole freaking town is fucking freaking out, Joy thought. Everyone's either inside the Coffee Shoppe getting pushed out by the St. Izzy's Keystone cop squad or they're lined up on the sidewalk looking in through the window.

Amanda had the same thought.

The Chronicle's two crack reporters, the journalists who specialized in finding the missing, nodded and winked at each other as two of St. Isidore's finest not so gently pushed through the Coffee Shoppe's door.

Of course, Amy and Joy offered only token resistance to the cops shoving them out the door. The women were more than happy to leave. There was work to be done, interviews that needed to take place, and most importantly, stories to write.

"We've written all we have about David and Hans," said Amanda.

"But now we need to do their obituaries and get comments from the survivors," Joy said.

"What about our Ms. Sullivan?"

"Oh she's the real story," Joy said with a smile. "That'll take both of us. But first, we have to find out who she was. Then we can find out where she is."

"Okay, how did she get out of town so fast?"

"Exactly, and where did Mary Eileen go? We know she didn't vanish."

"If we can find her before the cops?"

"That will be so huge."

"So fucking huge."

"Yeah, so let's say you wanted to get out of St. Isidore fast," Joy said, flashing her eyes at Amanda to stop the snarky, sarcastic answer that was forming on her lips. "Okay, you killed somebody, maybe a couple of somebodies. How do you get out of town fast?"

"You don't have a car?"

"Or you don't want to take your car?"

"Too easy to trace, right."

"Who do you call?"

There was only one choice in St. Isidore. But it was an excellent choice, Joy and Amanda had to admit when the answer to the question came to them simultaneously.

"Uber!" Amanda and Joy nearly shouted before they quieted each other with fingers to lips. The last thing they wanted was for the cops to hear their conclusion.

Amanda nibbled playfully on Joy's finger as her mentor whispered, "Let's call Uber."

Twenty One

Even without a finger to nibble, Sean had the same thought. It wasn't rocket science. It was a homicide investigation. And, while there was a lot to be said for forensic science and computers and analytics; Sean knew nothing would ever replace one-on-one, face-to-face contact.

There were two kinds of people in the world: those who liked to talk to the cops and feel like they had a role in solving crimes and those who were afraid of the police fearing a detective would figure out they had a part in committing a crime.

Sean found a member of the former community on the street outside the Coffee Shoppe.

"Hey. man, if I wanted to get out of here fast, I mean really fast, how would I do it?" Sean said a millisecond after flashing his silver shield in the face of a middle-aged dude who had 'cop wannabe' written all over his face. Surrounded by crime scene tape as he was, the brand "I wanna be a cop" was nearly glowing on his forehead.

"I'd call Uber," Adam King said. It was true that the one thing he wanted to do more than anything else in the world, at least in his former life, was to be a cop. He had everything it took except the physical strength. Adam couldn't do a pull-up if his life depended on it. The St. Isidore Police Department let him volunteer every once in a while for parades and that kind of thing. But he had washed out of a paid job on the force.

While, Adam was in love with his lady, Anne, and satisfied with his business, The Reading Room, he still was thrilled to have a conversation with a real homicide detective.

houses. That seemed so odd, but then Mary Eileen remembered what her customers from this side of Michigan had said about Detroit.

"Nobody lives there anymore."

However, Mary Eileen knew that was wrong if only because of the police, fire and ambulance sirens that punctuated her fear.

Once she got used to their shrillness, the sounds of emergency vehicles seemed comforting. At least there are police in the area, Mary Eileen thought. As long as they don't know who I am, I can go to them for help if I need it.

But she also knew that once she contacted a cop, the first thing any officer of the law would do would be to check her background, and get her story, by asking for her DOB, her date of birth, and running it on the computer.

If the lunkheads at St. Izzy P. D. found their way to the state police computer, Mary Eileen Sullivan knew she might as well put a gun to her head and pull the trigger. She'd seen state police cars coming into St. Isidore as she was driving out. The local police, Mary Eileen could handle. Hell, she'd killed two men, disposed of their bodies, and the cops never asked her more than the most rudimentary questions as part of a missing person investigation. But she knew the state police were on another plateau of law enforcement. Those guys are good, Mary Eileen thought. She had to stay off their radar screen.

Once she got settled, Mary Eileen knew she could walk into any coffee shop in Detroit and make enough money under the table to survive. All she needed was a roof over her head. A hot shower would be nice, too. Her phone's battery was just about dead. An electrical outlet would also be nice.

There seemed to be no better plan than to start knocking on doors and trying door knobs. If these houses were empty, there was no reason Mary Eileen couldn't at least spent the night inside away from the bad guys and away from the police.

Tomorrow, she would find a coffee shop. At least Mary Eileen could find a job. She'd offer to work under the table, all cash, no benefits. She'd have taken on that kind of an employee in St. Isidore; hell, she did. Christina was a total illegal alien. No papers, no nothing. Mary Eileen could be the same kind of person, completely illegal, a non-existent person with absolutely no record of ever being alive.

But first, she needed to get off the street.

Mary Eileen was no cat burglar. She had never broken into a home in her life, but that is just what she knew she had to do on this miserable broken-down street in Detroit.

Not knowing what else to do she just knocked at the front door of the first home. No one answered, "Obviously, not at home," she thought to herself.

Mary Eileen crept along the side of the house. It had once been a beautiful home. It wasn't anymore, but once, it must have been a sight to behold.

I'll bet they all were really something back about a century ago, Mary Eileen thought.

Four, no five stories tall, she noted. Mary Eileen couldn't be sure of course, but if this house were in Great Britain, it would've gone up somewhere been the mid-nineteenth century and the first year of the twentieth century.

"When that grand old lady, Queen Victoria, was on the throne," Mary Eileen said aloud. She had to keep talking. It quieted her fears. She'd survived and even thrived in New York's Times Square and Manhattan. It was also true she grew up in Belfast, but she fled as soon as she could. And Belfast, as bad as it was, had not been anything like what she saw around her in Detroit.

Yet, Mary Eileen felt somewhat at home. She was standing outside a house in a Victorian neighborhood. Patterned bricks, terraces, decorated roof line, and slates; the houses on this street had it all. But those blocks that probably came from one of the brickyards in St. Isidore back in the late 1800s and set in what was known back then as a Flemish Brick Bond — bricks with an end pointing out at the street that alternated with bricks that showed their long side — had long since started falling out. The mortar had turned to sand. The lush gardens that had grown so splendidly on the front and rear of the homes had gone to weeds years ago, and what was left of the mosaic stained glass windows had been smashed by stone-throwing vandals.

While Mary Eileen saw the damage, she felt homesick for Ireland.

"I'll bet they even have a fireplace in every room," Mary Eileen whispered to herself.

Wait! A light had just popped on in a home across the street. Mary Eileen scurried across the road, not bothering to look for traffic. Getting hit by a car, she thought, would be a small problem. At least then she could find a place to bed down in a hospital emergency room.

However, she did run half-bent-over like a soldier running through incoming gunfire. Once on the other side of the street, Mary Eileen caught her breath, straightened her clothes and walked erect, fully confident, intending to knock on the front door, announce herself and plead for help, until another gunshot rang out.

Mary Eileen immediately dove to the ground. Her face was in a muddy patch, at least she hoped it was nothing more toxic than mud. She was flat on her belly but managed to raise her hands in what she hoped was a sign of surrender.

Mary Eileen risked raising her head to look at the house.

All that produced was another gunshot. Whoever was shooting missed Mary Eileen again, but the bullet hit the sidewalk behind her and ricocheted off into the night.

Mary Eileen rolled three times through the mud and weeds that made up the front yard of the home. She got up on her hands and knees, looked at the house again and this time saw the barrel of a rifle poking out of a second-story window.

There was only one option. No Plan B or Plan C. There was only Plan A: Run. And that is just what Mary Eileen did. She ran like never before until she heard the music.

Twenty Three

Sean instinctively ducked when he heard the gunshot. Had to be a rifle, he thought, being an expert on guns. He was a state police marksman and had done a couple of years as a sniper in hostage negotiations, so if there was one thing Sean knew, it was the sound of a rifle.

But this weapon, whose sound echoed down the street of beat-up gingerbread houses wasn't a modern gun. He was betting it might be one of the rifles that were used to win the West, maybe 200 years ago; a Winchester. That meant the person who fired it wasn't a professional hit man, not even a professional criminal. Probably just an old bum who was living in one of these rat traps, Sean decided.

Normally this guy wouldn't be worth worrying about, but even an idiot could fire a rifle.

Sean also knew that whoever it was firing that rifle, he or she, undoubtedly kept an eye on everything that moved on this street. He was someone Sean wanted to speak with as soon as possible.

The Uber driver, who had driven Mary Eileen first up to the Upper Peninsula and then down the length of Michigan to Detroit, had been very forthcoming. Once Sean ran a background check and found out the guy was a convicted sex offender — nobody dangerous, just dumb enough to have exposed himself as a teenager to some little girls — and had not reported his latest change of address; it wasn't hard to persuade him to exchange information for freedom.

So unless the Uber driver lied, and he might have, Mary Eileen had been on this street a little more than a week ago. She might still be here. Sean had to find out, and the easiest way to do that would be a little face-to-face time with whoever had that rifle.

"Jeez," said Sean as he hit the ground to avoid a ricocheting bullet. He had stood up to draw fire never expecting the rifleman to be such a good shot. Fortunately for Sean, the shooter had not been good enough, and he was able to spot the muzzle flash.

Sean did an Army crawl on his elbows and knees to get to the side of the house. There was no way he could use the front door. Even the back door would be too dicey. The guy was firing out of a second-story window facing the street. Sean needed to get behind him, but the door would be too obvious. If this guy turned out to be some urban survivalist, he might have wired a booby trap to the back door. Could be a small homemade bomb — it was easy enough to figure out how to make one of those with a quick search of the internet — or it might be a good, old-fashioned, trip-shotgun with a wire running from the trigger to the door. Whoever opened the back door would either get himself blown up or catch a load of lead in the face.

Sean didn't see himself coming out of either scenario alive, so he decided to use a window.

He crawled to the side of the house and found an old garden shed set up against the side of the home. The old, Victorian houses in the neighborhood had each been surrounded with gardens back in the days when Detroit was prospering. Having a shed closest to one of the areas where the homeowners, or their staff, were working on the gardens made perfect sense.

Sean found a couple of old tires in the backyard, rolled them over to the shed, put one on top of the other and climbed onto the shed's roof. He wasn't worried about the rifleman. Sean was confident that the shooter had missed him crawling through the high grass and weeds that surrounded the Victorian mansion. There was no reason for him to take his eyes of the street. The gunman had to be figuring that if his target had escaped getting shot and somehow did make it to the backyard, he'd be taken out by whatever bobby trap he'd designed from a survivalist's website.

Looking overhead, Sean saw a long, orange cord running from one of the power poles three houses away to a window about six feet over the shed.

"Nice, he found a source of energy," Sean said to himself. "This guy knows what he's doing."

So he did have a survivalist in the house. Sean ratcheted up his approach. Once inside, he would not be dealing with a wimp. Chances are this guy would put him down without thinking twice. There's no way he'd be able to ID Sean as a cop. Wearing an old t-shirt and jeans, with a revolver in his ankle holster and a Glock wedged in his jeans in the back, Sean was armed and ready. But he certainly didn't look like law enforcement. He had his ID, but Sean was sure this guy would never give him a chance to pull out his badge. Even if Sean hung it around his neck, the guy would shoot first and check the silver shield second.

Sean couldn't blame him. He'd do the same thing. But that didn't mean Sean wanted to die.

Once on top of the shed, Sean knew he had to move fast. As sturdy as it might have been in its day, there had to be some wood rot. A paint brush hadn't touched it in forever. Sean was confident it wouldn't hold him for long. But now that he was on top of it, Sean could see into one of the rooms. Almost feeling the old shed swaying under his weight, Sean used the blade of the hunting knife he had in a sheath on his belt to pry open the wood window.

It took some effort. Sean was glad he'd kept up with the shoulder and back weight machines in the state police gym. He needed every bit of strength he had to slide the window up.

That was another sign this guy, this survivalist or whatever he was, was no dummy. The window hadn't been painted shut. Mr. Have Rifle Will Travel might want to get out of the house sometime as much as Sean wanted to get in that night. A painted-tight window was something he would not have wanted to force open.

Sean was glad of that. But it also increased his alert factor by a couple of digits. He was moving in on a professional, or at least somebody who excelled in this business of staying alive. He'd have to be to survive the urban combat in Detroit; Sean thought to himself as he landed lightly inside what had been a bedroom.

He heard a shell being racked into shotgun behind him as he reached back for his Glock. The double-barrels of the rifle pressed against his back. Right between the shoulder blades. If the guy, or girl, with the gun, squeezed the triggers it would rip Sean in two. His arms would go to the right and left, his head was fly up in the air, and his chest would splatter across the room against the paint that was peeling off the wall about ten feet away.

The guy with the gun, Sean was assuming he was a male if only because men were much more likely than women to be able to wield a shotgun — and Sean had no time to worry about being politically correct. But the gunman had made a critical mistake. Sean was still on the balls of his feet. The gunman had not pushed him down to his knees. That meant Sean was completely balanced. His weight was perfectly centered. The sensation of the over-and-under barrels of that gun against Sean's back was just what he wanted.

Sean's left foot was to the front, his right to the rear. Just as the rifle pressed against his back, Sean shifted his weight to his back foot and pivoted to his right. He swung his right arm to knock the gun away from his back and his left to grab the barrel before the startled gunman could fire.

Sean snatched the gun away as quickly as stealing candy from a baby. As a matter of fact, it was much easier. His little brother had put up much more of a fight. So had his sister.

Sean completed the spin, whipped the shotgun around and brought it into firing position. Standing before Sean was a skinny, long-haired, t-shirt and jeans wearing, barefoot, bearded man with absolutely no upper body strength. Sean couldn't help smirking as he raised his eyebrows and without saying a word ordered the man to drop to his knees.

Sean held on to the shotgun with his right hand and used his left to pull his badge on a chain out from beneath his shirt. The man's eyes grew wide. But they shouldn't have. The authority of law enforcement oozed from every pour in Sean's body. He was the man. Who could doubt it? Certainly not the punk in front of him.

Sean didn't say a word. He just pulled a folded-up picture of Mary Eileen out of his pocket, showed it to the man, and took his nodding head as a "yes." Sean Patrick Flynn had found his woman.

Twenty Four

Detroit was a big city. Even with its post-Great Recession Exodus, The Big D was easily eight times the size of St. Isidore. But Amanda was confident they could find Mary Eileen with little trouble. Joy was not so sure.

"She's gotta eat, right?"

"This again?"

"Right, this again," Amanda said. "Mary Eileen has to eat. That means she had to make money."

"Of course, and how does she make money?" Joy knew she was entirely rhetorical. They'd had this conversation at least once a day for the week they'd been in Detroit.

"She makes coffee. She works in a coffee shop. She finds a coffee shop that will pay her under the table, not a Starbucks or anything like that, and Mary Eileen makes enough money to live."

"You might be giving her an awful lot of credit," Joy said.

"All we have to do is find that kind of coffee shop," said Amanda.

"And you might be giving us an awful lot of credit, too."

Still, Joy had to admit they had two weeks to do their investigation, and only one week was gone. Esther Shapiro, who'd taken over day-to-day management of the Chronicle was like a born-again believer when it came to the power of Joy and Amanda to bring in stories.

Why wouldn't she be? The Chronicle's dynamic duo had found the basement where a serial killer had been hiding his victims, all young women, before taking them out to hang in the Suicide Forest. True, they were not able to rescue the woman and couldn't make a case against the killer, a high school teacher of all people, but they had found the basement and had written a hell of a story.

And that was just the first of the missing person, cold-case style stories Joy and Amanda had tackled.

Esther had been nearly as confident as Amanda when she granted them two weeks and pretty much carte blanche when it came to the Chronicle's credit card to work this case in Detroit.

"The upside potential is tremendous," Esther said. "Think of the splash you two could make."

Joy put one hand over her face and held Amanda's hand with the other as they held on tight for another tidal wave of corporate business speak.

"Here we have a woman who's probably killed at least two guys — an ex-husband and a boyfriend — cut up their bodies, encased them in cement and hidden them in her basement," Esther gushed. "Good God, how could it be any better?"

"Wait, wait, don't tell me," Amanda said.

All aboard, Joy thought, now she's using the name of Esther's favorite radio show. Is Amanda's nose turning brown, or is she just using lots of butter to grease the skids, Joy wondered.

"Right, there is only one way it could be better," Esther said. "And that way would be for the St. Isidore Chronicle's Spotlight staff, you and Joy, to find this serial killer and run her to ground."

Well, no business cliches, Joy thought, but I think Esther's been reading some serious crime books.

Whatever the source of her enthusiasm, she decided there was no better train to ride than this one that was obviously going to pull out of the station with or without the lovely Joy Ellis.

So like any reporter would do when offered a company credit card and car, she jumped on board.

And off they went, she and Amanda, to Detroit to find Mary Eileen Sullivan, a serial killer.

And now here they were, in Detroit, preparing to locate the coffee shop where their prey might or might not be working, and hopefully, they would "run her to ground," Joy winced as she remembered Esther's line, without getting themselves cut up and stuffed in a cement overcoat.

Joy had been reading some crime novels, too.

A COUPLE OF HOURS AFTER they hit the Motor City, Joy had to admit Amanda had been right. It was easy enough of find potential coffee shops on the internet. And thanks to the Uber dispatcher looking for some quick fame in the pages of the Chronicle, the driver had refused to talk, they had a pretty good idea of the neighborhood where Mary Eileen would be hanging out, trying to survive.

But tromping from one coffee shop to the next — the Espresso Bar, the Final Grind, the Brewer, the Roaster, the White Pigeons, Jack's Warm Buns and of course, Central Perc— the list of places selling and roasting coffee was endless.

Joy and Amanda spent a week going from one coffee bar to the next.

"I can't take one more espresso," Amanda said holding her stomach as she and Joy walked through the door of a place called Bean There, Brewed That.

"At least the owner seems more creative than the last ten or twelve," said Joy. But she had to admit that her stomach turned at just the thought of one more latte.

"If we don't find Mary Eileen by the end of the day, I say we turn around and go back home," Joy said.

"If we find her today, I think I will just kill her and spare the court system the trouble," muttered Amanda.

"Don't you dare!" Joy said as she pushed the door open and saw one more brick inside wall in one more coffee shop. "This story is our ticket to New York! I can hear CNN calling right now."

"Okay, okay. Calm down," Amanda said.

The women, St. Isidore Chronicle's Dynamic Duo backed out of the doorway to let a young couple — two men, both with neatly trimmed beards and a definite bounce in their step, walk out hand-in-hand.

Joy was just about to whisper to Amanda, "We aren't in St. Isidore anymore," when she saw her. Mary Eileen Sullivan in all her Irish glory, auburn tresses tied in a neat bun, green eyes flashing, turned around from the coffee bar with a tray of steaming hot drinks on her shoulder.

Good, God! Amanda and Joy shared the thought as they spun on tip-toe and looked at each other with the smile of conspirators whose master plan was about to pay off.

The next moment they shared another thought — Oh My God! — as two male hands grabbed each of their shoulders from behind and pulled them out of Bean There, Brewed That.

"What the fuck?" Amanda managed to say as she tried to wriggle out from the grasp of a man whose hand was as big and hairy as a bear's paw. She looked up over her shoulder and saw a giant with blond hair and blue eyes. Irish? A friend of Mary Eileen's? Amanda wondered.

Joy was twisting and squirming herself. The guy who had her wasn't nearly as tall or cute. But he was a muscular as anyone Joy had ever encountered. Her brothers had push some real crushing grips on her during childhood wrestling matches, but this guy was almost crushing her collarbone.

He used his other hand, as did Amanda's abductor, to grab one of Joy's wrists and twist it behind her back.

The men pulled and then pushed Amanda and Joy away from the coffee shop and into an alley behind Bean There, Brewed That.

As much as they had been dreading their next shot of caffeine a few moments ago, Joy and Amanda were both wishing they could have just one more coffee before getting a shot of whatever these two had planned for them.

Two big, black SUVs — the kind of trucks that were either used by politicians or awful bad guys in the movies — were parked about 100 feet away. Amanda and Joy sensed both of those vehicles had trouble inside.

"Do you realize who we are?" Joy said as Amanda cringed. She had never been in this kind of situation before, and she always gave deference to her boss and mentor. But really Joy, is this the best play to make, Amanda couldn't help thinking.

"We are reporters for the St. Isidore Chronicle," Amanda said. It was probably best to play along now that Joy had tossed down the first card.

"If we go missing, people will be looking for us," Joy said, making the next obvious play.

But who were these guys? The journalistic souls of Joy and Amanda begged for an answer. It's not like they had any real money. Were they being kidnapped? Or could it be that Mary Eileen had a couple of cohorts who were protecting her?

Maybe this story was even bigger than they thought.

"Someone's looking for you already," said one of the men holding Joy. He pulled her around to the driver's side of one of the SUVs and opened the passenger door for the rear seat. The other one pulled the rear passenger door on the other side and pushed Amanda inside.

The engine was running, as was the air conditioner. The atmosphere was almost as chilly as one might expect for a final ride, Joy thought. Even in this moment of utter fear she couldn't help composing an article in her head.

Amanda was chewing on her lip. Her protege seemed so, well, tiny, helpless and even vulnerable that Joy reached over and held her hand, trying to reassure Amanda that everything would be okay.

But Joy knew that chances were worse than 50-50 that they would survive.

Two men sat in the front. It was easy to see from the size of the backs of their heads that they were big guys and even muscular. Their necks were next to nothing. It was almost like they had to skulls mounted on swiveling pedestals.

Amanda was scared to death. They had been in tight situations before, tracking serial killers, homicidal maniacs and even white-collar criminals who might kill before they allowed themselves to be dragged away to prison. But this was the first time someone had gotten the drop on them, to quote the pulp crime novels Joy loved to read.

Amanda looked at the guys in the front seat and just knew either one of them could snap her like a twig.

The man in the passenger seat put his hand to his mouth and cleared his throat. He seemed to be dressed in business casual and was wearing a brown sports coat. The attire gave Amanda and Joy at least a little hope.

He cleared his throat and turned to his left.

Amanda and Joy blinked hard and looked at each other with their mouths hanging open and their eyebrows dancing.

"Joy and Amanda," Sean Patrick Flynn said as he smiled and nodded at each woman, "what a pleasant surprise."

Twenty Five

Bean There, Brewed That. It was a name so smart that Mary Eileen almost wished she had thought of it for her coffee shop. But that didn't matter as much as getting off her feet. She must have walked a mile from the rats and other vermin, like her new boyfriend, who infested the mansion that Mary Eileen called home.

It was a combination of music and outright exhaustion that drove her down that street to the mansion with an orange electrical cord running into a window. She'd climbed on an old, rickety shed, using a couple of old tires to get close enough to the shed's roof to hop up and grab the ledge with her fingertips.

With a strength she had forgotten she had, Mary Eileen pulled herself onto the top of the shed, found a window open and shimmied inside. She wandered through the rooms, using the last bit of battery strength in her smartphone to run the flashlight app and avoid the mice and whatever else was scurrying on the floor, and the piles of clothes, books, furniture, and pictures.

The woodwork that had survived Detroit's Great Recession was spectacular; Mary Eileen had to admit. During her exploration of the house, she would find four bathrooms, none of which with a functioning toilet, the water must have been cut off long ago.

She also found one man inside, or rather, he found her.

Mary Eileen was wandering down a hall on the third floor when she thought she heard the sound of footsteps behind her. Oh, fuck, she thought. This is not going to end well. Not unless I can use all my powers, Mary Eileen laughed to herself. She wasn't afraid of some bum in a shack. She'd dealt with worse, much worse, in New York.

The sound of a shell racked into a shotgun wrecked her confidence. This guy is more serious than most, Mary Eileen thought. Or maybe he is more afraid than I am Mary Eileen decided to use a weapon she had not unveiled in days, and perhaps one Mr. Shotgun Man hadn't seen in an every long time. Mary Eileen turned and smiled. And they reached what could be called, an agreement.

Now Mary Eileen had a place to call home while she reinvented herself. True, she had to do more for this guy — she did almost feel sorry for him, living along for a year scared to death of whatever or whoever came down the street at night — than she had wanted to do. But this arrangement gave her the space she needed. And it's not like Mary Eileen had never traded favors.

Jason — that was his name — had everything she needed. This guy was hunkered down for the duration of whatever warfare came to him in Detroit. Thanks to his power-stealing orange electrical cord that ran from the house to a power pole, they had a refrigerator, a TV, radio; and even a computer. Since Mary Eileen had Verizon data, she didn't need a Wi-Fi connection for her smartphone. She was all set. Yeah, running water would have been nice. But Jason had a garden hose running through three backyards to a house where the water was on. At night, they'd turn on the tap and run back through the yards to collect as much water as possible in the three bathtubs in the house.

So Mary Eileen would live.

Making a living was next. There had to be coffee shops, right? It was a simple matter to find one that would pay her under the table. Once she plugged her phone into Jason's computer to recharge it, Mary Eileen searched for small coffee shops, the independents, who must be struggling.

Mary Eileen knew first hand the trials, tribulations and financial margins of running a coffee shop. Everybody thought selling a four-dollar cup of coffee made with probably a nickel's worth of beans should be like having a license to print money.

How little they knew about all of the other expenses that went into running any small business. Mary Eileen knew. And she also realized that anyone facing the challenges she had faced in the Coffee Shoppe might be willing to do just what she had done — hire someone ready to work without bennies, somebody, who wanted to stay under the radar and get paid under the table.

And, so she found herself at Bean There, Brewed That. Not a bad gig. She was making a few hundred dollars a week, all tax free, no questions asked.

Had Mary Eileen spent time thinking about Sean? Sure, she did. This guy she was with, this Jason, was such a nothing compared to Sean. Mary Eileen had to close her eyes and think about the one true love of her life every night that Jason took her to bed.

She had not resisted. She had even pretended. Mary Eileen needed this guy and this house. She didn't have a master plan for the reinvention of herself yet. All Mary Eileen required was time, some money and if things kept going the way they were, a chainsaw and a bag of cement mix wouldn't hurt either.

So far though, Jason was serving his purpose. So Jason was still alive. And he would breathe as long as he was a good boy and didn't ask for too much. Still, he was on thin ice. Now that Mary Eileen had a good job or at least a way to bring in money without selling her body she really didn't need Jason. She could buy her food. She could protect herself. His guns could quickly become her weapons. And Mary Eileen still had the Beretta that she'd used to free herself from David and Hans.

Jason could be next.

Later for that, Mary Eileen decided. She'd had enough drama in her life the past few weeks. If nothing else, Jason was a life support system for an adequate penis.

And as long as she dreamed of Sean, the pretending part wasn't so bad.

"White mocha latte, two dark coffees, and three muffins," Mary Eileen heard herself say to the Bean There bartender. As she waited for her order, her mind drifted, and she glanced out the front window watching the traffic and day dreaming.

Mary Eileen thought about Sean so hard at times like this; she could almost see him.

This morning, she was sure she had, at least twice. Mary Eileen had been thinking about Sean more than usual for the past couple of hours. Her last dream of the night, one that ended just before her smartphone's alarm went off at 4 a.m., was a rough one. It had been about Sean. The two of them were together. Mary Eileen couldn't remember all the particulars, but it had not ended well. She rubbed the sleep out of her eyes and laid in her sleeping bag for nearly ten minutes filled with a dread that comes when one realizes it could be a very, very rough day ahead.

Mary Eileen might have been able to rub the sleep out of her eyes, but she couldn't cleanse her mind of that dream. So, it was no wonder that every other guy who walked into Bean There, Brewed That looked for a moment just like Sean. Mary Eileen could have even sworn she had seen him in an SUV that rolled slowly by the store as she was opening for the morning.

But of course, there was no chance of that. He had to be teaching his literature students in Ann Arbor.

"It's a school day, right?" Mary Eileen whispered to herself.

Twenty Six

Sean didn't say anything. The women in the back seat were frozen as solid as a couple of chicken breasts hidden in the freezer behind the frozen vegetables that nobody wanted. He just smiled and flipped up his wallet that showed his state police badge and his identification. With the practice of years of shocking surprised suspects and witnesses, Sean held his badge and picture-ID next to his smiling face.

There could be no mistake. He was a cop. And not just a cop, Sean Patrick Flynn was a state police detective.

"What the fuck?" Amanda and Joy mouthed to each other silently.

"Well, said, ladies, well said," Sean said with a laugh. His partner in the front turned to his right so he could see the shock on the faces of their passengers.

"It seems we've been after the same person," Sean said, closing his ID.

"Could we see your ID, again?" Joy said.

Sean smiled and handed his wallet to them.

"Good God," Amanda said. "Sean Patrick Flynn, you're not a professor from Dublin."

"Are you even Irish?" Joy whispered.

"Well, Irish-American. My family came over in the 1800s, so there is some connection to Ireland, but I was born and bred in the suburbs of Detroit," Sean said. "And as for being a professor, hell, I hardly made it through four years at Wayne State and then the state police academy."

"But, Sean..." Amanda said.

"Why don't you just call me, detective," Sean said. "I mean, just so we all know who is in charge here, okay?"

What could Amanda and Joy do except shrug and nod their agreement? Who were they to complain. Their story had just gotten even better.

Amanda had an idea.

"Okay, Sean," Amanda said, dragging out his name until she ran out of breath.

"So you're an undercover cop, or you were until your cover just got blown," Joy said.

"What's next?" said Amanda.

Joy didn't chime in with her voice. She just lifted her eyebrows and waited.

"How did you find her? Was it luck, or are you just that fucking good?" said Amanda

"A little of both," said Sean. He could have shared his story of how he found Mary Eileen's new home, her faux boyfriend and how he convinced the pitiful excuse for a male to rat out his chick. But he chose not too. There would be plenty of time for that tale in court. Sean didn't have a minute to spare talking to reporters. He and his three-man squad of state police heavies were all on the clock. And their suspect had shown she could vanish in an instant.

It was time to bring Mary Eileen Sullivan home to St. Isidore.

"Stay here," Sean said.

Joy just about jumped out of her seat.

"No fucking way! This is our story," she said.

"Story? Who gives a flying fuck about your story?" said Sean's partner behind the SUV's steering wheel.

"Come on," said Amanda, "this could be excellent for you and the department. It's a great story to tell."

Sean laughed.

"No fucking way, who?"

"I meant, 'No way, detective.'"

He paused for a moment if only to insert his authority back into the conversation.

"Stay here," said Sean using a tone of voice that left no doubt there were plenty of handcuffs to go around if either Amanda or Joy should choose not to obey a direct order from a state police detective.

Again, Sean paused. This time he wanted to be sure the order had sunk in with both women. The last thing he needed was to have them go rogue on him while his men were bringing in a double-murderer.

Sean would have liked to have waited until Mary Eileen got off work and was walking home. But Joy and Amanda didn't leave him any choice. Well, there was a choice. If they waited like good cops should until Mary Eileen was free of any civilians who might get caught in an ugly crossfire, they would be stuck with two reporters in the back seat. Nearly a fate worse than death, Sean decided.

Besides, as dangerous as Mary Eileen might be, he was pretty confident that the element of surprise — Sean could hardly wait to see her face when he walked into Bean There — would give him all the advantage he would need.

Was he happy to bring this to a close? Yeah, Sean was pleased It was tough doing the undercover role of a literature professor making a play for a beautiful Irish girl, a real Colleen, who he wanted in actual life, not in his undercover life. No ruse, no fooling, just hot, hard lust and then love. Sean was head over heels in love with Mary Eileen Sullivan.

But he had always been a cop first. And so Sean was today. He was a cop who had to make an arrest. And, it was an arrest that would look good, damn good, on his record. So as he got out of the SUV and signaled to his men that it was time to go, Sean understood the meaning of the word 'bittersweet.' He could almost hear Michael Douglas defining the word in "Wall Street," as being "like watching your mother-in-law go off a cliff in your brand new Maserati."

His team, three of the sharpest, toughest uniforms on the street were standing with him. He had a great squad. They had brought in some significant cases, and this arrest would be right up there with the cream of that crop.

"Let's go," he said.

Two of the cops went into the coffee bar, first, while Sean and the trooper who had been behind the driver's wheel waited outside, out of sight. Once they got a table, they had to hold on, the place was packed, they chilled.

"Do you see here?" said Cop #1

"Yeah, she's right there," said his partner with a nod toward the serving station where the waitresses placed their orders.

Coming this way, #1 texted to Sean who was waiting by the SUV.

It was the best of both worlds for this arrest. Not only was Mary Eileen coming their way, she was also going to walk to the table occupied by two of the best state cops in the business.

They smiled. Mary Eileen smiled. Everyone was happy. But not for long.

Once Sean got the text from his men inside, he and his partner quickly walked to the front door.

Come in now, read the next text.

And that is just what they did. Sean moved behind Mary Eileen. He hesitated. Sean wanted to remember Mary Eileen as a free woman, before she became a criminal suspect on her way to jail, a woman on trial, and then a woman serving a double life sentence for two murders.

He wanted to remember the Mary Eileen that he had fallen in love with, not Mary Eileen the criminal.

She looked over her shoulder, almost with a sense of dread, almost knowing that the something she sensed would go wrong this morning was about to happen.

Mary Eileen saw Sean's eyes first. Then she registered the rest of his face. He was smiling. But it was a stiff, tense smile, not the smile of a lover who had found the one he loved, ready to begin a new life together.

No, Mary Eileen sensed Sean wasn't waiting for a latte. She knew he was there to tell her that it would soon be time for her to reinvent herself one more time. But this time, she would do it behind the walls of a prison.

Sean was just as handsome as she remembered him. Oh hell, it hadn't been that long since Mary Eileen had run away from St. Isidore. Still, it seemed like a lifetime. And in a way it was. Every time she reinvented herself, Mary Eileen felt like she started a new life.

Oh, how she had wanted to start a new life with this man, this Sean Patrick Flynn.

But it was not to be. Mary Eileen felt like she was outside her body watching all of this play out on a TV screen.

He showed her his badge. The men at the table got up behind her. Another man appeared at Sean's shoulder. Mary Eileen knew they were all cops. She knew that one way or another it was time to pay for every mistake she had made, every crime she had committed.

Sean read Mary Eileen her rights. He Mirandized her as they would say on the TV crime shows that had taught Mary Eileen so much about her craft. She saw his lips moving, but even though she nodded her head to indicate she understood, Mary Eileen hadn't heard what Sean had said.

The cops behind her grabbed her arms and put them behind her so they could put the handcuffs on her wrists. Sean moved to her side, took her by the arm and prepared to lead Mary Eileen out the door and to the SUV that was waiting to take her to jail.

Mary Eileen held firm. She didn't budge. Mary Eileen didn't take a step. Sean moved to face her.

"When did you know?" she said.

"I always knew."

"And still you fell in love with me?"

"It is time to go."

"I'm pregnant."

Twenty Seven

Amanda and Joy were positively awestruck when they saw Sean and Mary Eileen coming out of Bean There. Joy immediately unleashed her smartphone, an Android with an excellent camera, to take some pictures. Amanda started texting Chronicle headquarters with the bulletin..."Mary Eileen Sullivan arrested in Detroit. State police found her working in a coffee shop. She put up no resistance. Not a shot fired."

"Oh my God, is Sean bringing her to this car?" Joy said.

"We should be so lucky. Good, God! This is huge," Amanda fairly screamed in Joy's ear.

It was the story of a lifetime for both women. They were in on the arrest of St. Isidore's most notorious female serial killer. Joy and Amanda had found Mary Eileen at the same time state police arrived on the scene, so they could reasonably claim to have discovered Ms. Sullivan. Esther would have no problem making that stretch of journalistic license; both women were sure of that.

Thoughts of selling the story to a publisher and maybe even getting a movie deal ran rampant through their minds as Joy and Amanda watched Mary Eileen walk toward them with her hands behind her back. Sean was apparently holding her by the handcuffs. His fellow officers followed them. No one showed any signs of a struggle.

There was a bench seat behind Joy and Amanda that would have been perfect for Mary Eileen, but St. Isidore's favorite reporters didn't get that lucky.

A state police squad car, called by Sean from inside Bean There arrived to transport Mary Eileen back to a jail cell in Detroit. She would be processed, a lawyer would come, and the legal proceedings would begin.

When Mary Eileen did get back to St. Isidore there was little doubt as to her guilt or innocence. As a matter of fact, she not only confessed to Sean after he read the Miranda warning to her, Mary Eileen apologized.

"I know what I did was horrendous and wrong. I felt so miserable like I couldn't go on," Mary Eileen said. "I would have ended it all, but I didn't have the courage to kill myself."

The only question was, whether she knew what she was doing when she killed two men and disposed of their bodies, or if Mary Eileen had lost touch with reality and the difference between right and wrong.

Should prosecutors and the members of the jury feel a measure of pity for her as they might for anyone who suffered severe mental and emotional problems that left them incapable of functioning as a rational adult? Or should they consider her to be a cold, calculating, man-hating, serial killer?

JUST AS IT WAS THE story of a lifetime for Joy and Amanda, it was to be the court case of a career for St. Isidore County Assistant Prosecutor Patricia Fry.

Chief County Prosecutor Peter Logan could have taken the case himself, but with a woman on trial for her life, he felt the cause of justice — getting a conviction — would best be served if a woman handled the prosecution.

"It's mine?" Patricia Fry said. She was amazed to be getting the most famous, or infamous case in St. Isidore County's history. The only thing that beat it was the kidnapping of a young girl by a former high school teacher. The case never went to trial because police shot the suspect to death.

The case of Mary Eileen Sullivan was much different. While it was true there was no doubt that she was guilty, Mary Eileen had already confessed, Patricia knew that her lawyer, a sixty-seven-year-old wizard of the law, Michael Morris, could always throw her a curve ball and enter a plea of not guilty by reason of insanity.

Why am I getting this case? Patricia knew the answer without asking it aloud. Because I'm a woman, she thought. In a way that's insulting because if the suspect were a man and not a woman, I'd still be on midnight drunk tank duty.

"Of course, Logan could be setting me up to fail," Patricia told her BFF and roommate, Allyson.

"He is a pig. There's no doubt about that," Allyson replied. She and Patricia were on the same team — two women trying to make a career first, and a name for themselves second, in the St. Isidore County Prosecutor's Office. Both women were in their late twenties, Allyson was twenty-nine, Patricia was a year younger. And they were both from the Detroit area. St. Isidore seemed like such a second-class pop stand compared to the Motor City.

"But this is where we start, and we move up from here," Patricia would say whenever Allyson got down about it. Their classmates, most of them from the University of Michigan School of Law, had gone into either corporate or private practice, hanging out their own shingles. Allyson and Patricia had one more thing in common. They were raised by cops.

"They've got bad guys here, too," Patricia would remind her roommate. "We can do good work here."

And now she had a chance to do good work. Patricia could send a double murderer to prison for the rest of her life.

"I'm still worried this is going to be a lose-lose situation."

"How?"

"The best I can do is what everyone expects; life in prison without parole," Patricia said. "They just want a woman to put a woman behind bars. With me at the table, the defense won't have a chance to play the sexual discrimination card."

"So, cool. What's wrong with that? Use it to your advantage. You are woman, go ahead and roar."

"But if by some fluke Sullivan gets off, I am total burnt toast."

"That is true, girlfriend. That is true."

I could complain, and maybe I should, Patricia thought, chewing on her lip, but then where would I be? The answer was painfully obvious to her, back in Midnight Court with human vermin that were worse than homicidal; they were boring.

So, instead of complaining about the unfairness of being singled out to prosecute a woman just because she was female, Patricia sat literally on the edge of a chair in front of her mentor's desk two days later, and like any good student waited for him to speak.

Twenty Eight

Driving his state-issued Crown Vic through the narrow streets of downtown St. Isidore was more than a challenge for Sean, especially being as distracted as he was by the prospect of meeting with A.P. Fry.

"What does she need me for?" Sean asked his boss, State Police Commander Jack Hart.

"A.P. Fry says she needs your testimony; you testify. It's a simple as that."

"And my cover gets blown."

"Your cover gets blown, big fucking deal. This case is over. There isn't a soul in town who doesn't know you were sleeping with her."

Sean had to admit that Mary Eileen had done wrong. She had killed, not once but twice, and then she'd done her best to hide the evidence.

He also knew that as far as Commander Hart was concerned, his career as a state cop was close to being over. Sean had slept with the subject of a double-murder investigation. He might even be in love with her. It was all over the state police cop shop as well as every local law enforcement agency that had an internet connection. There was a good chance since loose lips can lift a career while sinking another, that somebody in blue would slip the story to one of the reporters running around St. Isidore.

If that happened, Sean was toast. He knew it. Hart knew it. And in a way, that was a very liberating feeling. "If it doesn't cost me anything to be generous, what the fuck, I might as well go all the way," Sean had told his reflection in the men's room mirror before going into Hart's office.

With the law-and-order fever that had taken over the nation, talk show pundits across America were calling for Mary Eileen's lifelong imprisonment. There was no way Sean was going to let that happen without a fight. If there was ever a doubt in his mind as to what he had to do, it was removed two days before his meeting with Hart when Sean saw Mary Eileen at the county jail.

Most prisoners shuffle to their side of a bulletproof glass partition that divides those in prison orange from their loved ones, friends, and attorneys. Mary Eileen didn't shuffle. She glided. Even though she'd been in a jail cell with three other women for the past thirty days, Mary Eileen Sullivan had not lost her sense of style.

Sean was amazed. She was the one he loved. Sean had admitted that to himself a couple of days before, but it was driven home when he saw Mary Eileen from the other side of the glass. And she was carrying his child. Mary Eileen was several months along now. Her baby bump was showing.

She smiled. Sean smiled. Their hands met on opposite side of the glass partition. It was the only thing that kept Sean and Mary Eileen apart.

"How is it?"

"I've been better."

"You look good."

"Liar."

It was a lie. A bruise under Mary Eileen's left eye had not healed, nor had the scratch marks on her cheek. Sean noticed the knuckles on her right hand were swollen and raw.

"The other woman looks worse?"

"Much."

"They want me to testify."

"I know."

"I can't."

"Yes, you can. You will."

Sean took a breath. He sat up straighter.

"I'll wait for you."

Mary Eileen smiled and began to stand. She took her hand from the glass, kissed her fingertips and blew the kiss to Sean. They both knew he might have to wait for the rest of his life before he could touch her again.

Fuck professionalism.

The skies over St. Isidore were cloudy, as usual. It had just rained. Nothing about the weather improved Sean's mood. But it certainly reflected his attitude. As Sean piloted the State Police Crown Vic through morning rush hour, he decided to do what he could to keep Patricia Fry at bay. Sean figured his career with the state police was over. There was no way he'd be able to get a job in law enforcement again. The cable TV people didn't know about him yet. But once Sean took the stand and began to tell his story; they'd be all over him like flies on shit.

Since his career was over, it wouldn't cost him a dime to be generous to the woman he loved. So what the fuck, why not go all the fucking way, Sean thought. Why not go all the fucking way?

Finding Assistant Prosecutor Patricia Fry's office was as much of a challenge as driving through downtown. After discovering the county courthouse, which was attached to city hall, Sean had to go up one escalator to the third floor, then walk down a hallway to an elevator and go up three more levels.

"Whoever built this monstrosity should be shot," Sean muttered under his breath.

The threat of violence didn't do much for the other three people in the elevator, all of whom were much smaller and far less intense than Sean. Two women and one man — who of course was afraid that if Sean got weird, it would be up to him to put him down — nervously looked at each for comfort as Sean tapped his fingers on the butt of his Glock.

One of the women sighed in relief when she noticed the gold State Police badge on Sean's belt.

It's not like Sean didn't know he'd made an impression on the three civilians and it did serve to lighten his mood. But he still dreaded the pre-trial conference set for nine a.m. with Patricia Fry.

She didn't keep him waiting long in the lobby. The Sullivan trial was the only thing on Fry's agenda for the next three months. Prosecutor Logan had cleared her calendar and assigned her drunk-tank detail to a couple of rookies fresh out of law school.

Being handed the Sullivan case, for whatever reason, was the break Patricia had been waiting for, but it still scared the hell out of her. If she dropped this ball, Patricia was only too aware that she'd never get another chance at any decent assignment.

Mary Eileen Sullivan's file was more than a last-chance career case. Patricia knew because of the national, and even international coverage this case was generating; her next step could be a statewide office, or even, not so far down the road, Congress. As long as she didn't blow it, this could be Patricia's ticket out of St. Isidore.

She had to go for life without parole. For Patricia to live her life to its fullest, Mary Eileen Sullivan was going to have to live hers in prison. This cop, Sean Patrick Flynn was going to have to live with it.

Twenty Nine

Patricia Fry's office door opened and a mountain of a man walked into her life. Sean Patrick Flynn was easily a foot taller that the assistant prosecutor and probably outweighed her by at least one-hundred pounds.

"Jesus, the guy is solid muscle," Patricia would tell Allyson that night.

"Tall?"

"Built."

"Hot?"

"Sizzling."

But that morning, Patricia couldn't let any of that show. It seemed like every guy in law school had been over six-feet-tall and was a total gym rat. Patricia had learned early on that is she gave an inch to these cavemen, they'd take everything she had.

Rather than stand up to shake Sean's hand, and be stuck looking up so high that she'd feel like she was falling over backward; Patricia stayed behind her desk and motioned Sean to take a seat.

"It was the only way I could look him in the eye," Patricia would tell Allyson while they worked on the last half of a bottle of Jack Daniels.

"If you stood?"

"I'd be looking right at his cock."

"Not where you wanted to be."

"Not this morning, that's for sure."

With Sean in the chair across from her desk, Patricia felt comfortable, at least more comfortable than she would have if she'd been in Sean's office.

The office is my turf, Patricia reminded herself. Even more than th courtroom, this is my neighborhood. And nobody fucks with me in my neighborhood.

She leaned back just a bit in her chair, but never lost eye contact, a she waited for Sean to speak.

"Ms. Fry..."

She raised her hand to stop Sean. Now, she had the advantage. Patricia was just where she wanted to be.

"Good morning, Detective Flynn. It is detective, right?"

Sean didn't answer. He was accustomed to being the one who aske the questions.

"Tell me about your investigation into the murders at the Coffe Shoppe. You went undercover, correct?"

"Yes, we began..."

"Did you fall in love with Mary Eileen Sullivan."

Hard as it is to believe a five-foot-three-inch, one-hundred-ten pound woman could slap a guy Sean's size hard enough to ring his bel Patricia Fry had just done it. Even the biggest fell to Mike Tyson. A verbal right hook delivered by Patricia has stopped Sean.

"Well..."

"Do you still love her?"

Sean was dazed. Again, he didn't respond while he tried to regai his bearings.

"Well?"

Sean took a breath.

"Well, what?"

"Did you love her?"

"Ms. Sullivan?"

"Yes, Detective Flynn. Ms. Sullivan. Mary Eileen Sullivan," Patrici said. "Who else would I be speaking of?"

Sean sat back in his chair. He broke eye contact. Sean looked ove Patricia's shoulder at what passed for the skyline of St. Isidore. Not single building over ten stories tall, most of them built when Michael Jackson was hot. On the wall to Patricia's left a couple of diplomas were in glass frames. Sean couldn't read the names of the schools, but he was willing to bet the word 'Harvard' didn't appear on either diploma.

There was a credenza under Flynn's credentials holding files stacked three deep.

Three bookshelves were on the wall to Patricia's right. Each held a few law books.

But in this whole office, Sean realized, there is not a single thing that was 'personal.' Outside of this office, Patricia Flynn had nothing that could be called a 'life.' At least no life that she cared to share with the rest of the county building.

Sean laughed.

"Yes, ma'am, she is why we are here." Sean knew her game now. Patricia Fry wanted to get out of St. Isidore as much as anyone with even a drop of ambition. She saw Mary Eileen's conviction as her exit visa.

Sean was not about to let that happen.

"Yes," he said.

"Yes, what?"

"Yes, I fell in love with her, and yes, I still love her." Oh, that felt good. Saying that aloud made Sean feel so much better.

What a morning!

Not only was it the first time he had admitted it to another member of the human race; it was the first time he had the courage to say it aloud.

"I do love Mary Eileen Sullivan."

"And that's professional?"

"Not sure it's in the manual."

"Are you going to be able to testify? Am I going to be able to count on you?"

"Of course I will and of course you will."

Patricia leaned back in her chair and crossed her arms. She'd let Flynn think about that for a minute. Would he be able to testify? Patricia had to be able to count on him. Sean was her key witness. If the defense attorney broke Sean, the case would fall apart, and Patricia would watch any chance she had of blowing this pop stand called St. Isidore sailing on a breeze out of the nearest courtroom window.

"So you are a state police detective, assigned to investigate a murder. You think you know who did it, at least Mary Eileen Sullivan was your leading suspect, correct?"

"Correct."

"But you fell in love with her."

"Yes."

"You fell in love with a murderer and not just any killer. She was a murderer who killed not one, but two men then cut up their bodies with a chainsaw, mixed cement and used it to hide each arm, leg, hand, foot, and head in the cellar under her coffee shop."

Sean leaned back in his chair and crossed his arms.

"That's about right, yeah. I think you've got that spot on."

Sean felt as good as when he admitted aloud that he loved Mary Eileen. Now he had told the world that he had fallen for a stone-cold killer; a woman who not only killed, she dismembered, she mutilated, and then she hid evidence.

If there ever was anyone who should spent the rest of their life in prison for what they had done, it was Mary Eileen Sullivan. Sean knew that. He was aware that Mary Eileen should pay the ultimate price. And if it were anyone but Mary Eileen Sullivan, Sean would volunteer to lock the cell door and throw away the key.

But they were talking about Mary Eileen Sullivan. So, there was no way Sean would let that happen. He was going to have to do whatever he could to derail Assistant Prosecutor Fry's case without committing perjury and without losing what little professional self-respect he had left.

Patricia smiled. She could read Sean's mind as easily as that of any criminal, which is exactly what he was as far as she was concerned. You want to help your girlfriend beat a murder charge, Patricia thought as she smiled across her desk at Sean. You want to beat me in court. Good luck with that.

Sean didn't scare her in the least. What did concern Patricia was the attorney who had offered to take Mary Eileen's case pro bono.

Thirty

Mary Eileen learned quickly that life in the Suicide Watch Wing of the St. Isidore County Jail was lonely. She'd been by herself for most of her time in New York, and even when employees and customers surrounded Mary Eileen at the Coffee Shoppe, she had felt alone.

David and Hans? Forget about those two, Mary Eileen thought to herself. The only time she had not been lonely when she was with Sean.

"I'll never see him again," Mary Eileen said to herself. Sean had told her differently when he visited, but Mary Eileen didn't believe him.

"He's a cop. I'm a killer. Why would he even consider being with me?"

Mary Eileen knew the guards were watching her through any of the cameras mounted in the four corners of her cell. They were probably counting the times she muttered to herself. But these days, who else did Mary Eileen have for conversation? True, there was the prison doctors who came to speak with her and she had a psychiatrist. But that was it. Mary Eileen's mistake had been admitting her guilt so quickly and then telling her cellmate that she would just as soon kill herself if she had the courage.

Mary Eileen was sitting on the floor hands around her knees which were pulled up to her chest, rocking gently and humming a song that her mother used to sing before they left Ireland.

Mary Eileen closed her eyes and began whispering the words of the lullaby.

Rest tired eyes a while
Sweet is thy baby's smile,

Angels are guarding
And they watch o'er thee.
Sleep, sleep, grah mo chree*
Here on your mamma's knee,
Angels are guarding
And they watch o'er thee,
The birdeens sing a fluting song
They sing to thee the whole day long,
Wee fairies dance o'er hill and the dale
For very love of thee.

The song made Mary Eileen think of the baby that was growing inside her. She'd gone through morning sickness. She felt okay now. But the depression was almost more than Mary Eileen could handle. If only she hadn't killed David and Hans. If only Sean had come along sooner. There didn't seem to be much more to live for except her baby. That's what kept her alive. That's what the doctors who put her in the Suicide Watch wing of the jail didn't understand. Mary Eileen was not about to kill herself, yet. If she didn't, there'd be another murder she'd have to account for; the death of Sean's baby.

It was lonely, but she did feel better in the Suicide Watch wing. It was so quiet and peaceful. However, even the jail itself had been much calmer and cleaner than Mary Eileen had imagined. She'd seen "Orange is the New Black," and the other prison shows on Netflix. She'd expected gangsters and lesbians would beat, rob and rape her. Instead, Mary Eileen's cellmate was a high school teacher who had sex with one of her students.

She was much more afraid of Mary Eileen Sullivan than Mary Eileen was of her. Kate McManus stayed in her bunk and didn't say a word for the first week. Then finally, either gathering courage or deciding that if Mary Eileen wanted to kill her, she'd already have been dead, Kate spoke.

"I liked the Coffee Shoppe. I stopped there almost every morning on my way to school."

Mary Eileen had recognized her as a regular. But, as with most of her customers, Mary Eileen had never bothered to ask her name. Just as she would have from behind the counter, Mary Eileen gave Kate a half-smile and nodded her thanks. Then came the question Mary Eileen knew Kate most wanted to ask; the question that Mary Eileen most needed to answer.

"Did you do it? Did you kill those men and cut up their bodies?"

And with that, Kate had opened the door to Mary Eileen's tearful, sobbing confession and admission that she'd commit suicide if only she had the courage.

"That's the problem with talking to people," Mary Eileen told herself as she rocked back and forth in her lonely cell. "They might just believe you. And worse yet; they just might tell someone else."

Mary Eileen stopped rocking. She didn't want to hurt the baby by pressing her knees against her stomach. As she was getting on her cot, her cell door opened. Two guards, one male, the other female, came into the cell, as Mary Eileen stood and silently accepted the cuffs and chains around her ankles and wrists.

She didn't bother to ask where they were going; Mary Eileen had learned in her first week that it didn't matter if she wanted to go or not. It was much easier to submit.

The first few times, Mary Eileen had fought back. Although she was not a large woman, the guards soon learned that Mary Eileen could put up quite a fight. That's why two guards now entered her cell together. No longer would a single female guard be given the task of watching over Mary Eileen.

Her violent behavior was also why Mary Eileen's meals were now brought to her three times a day. Even though the county jail was a relatively calm, yet confining, place; Mary Eileen had trouble with some of the other inmates. They had decided to see what she was made of and Mary Eileen had shown they quickly by driving her fingers into one woman's eyes. When a guard had gotten between them, Mary Eileen hit her throat so hard the larger woman had dropped like a rock.

Because of her pregnancy, the jail's full-time doctor decided she could not receive any tranquilizing medicine, so there was no alternative but to assign an extra guard to watch Mary Eileen and above all else, keep her away from the rest of the jail's inmate population.

As they walked down first one hallway and then turned left down another, Mary Eileen kept her eyes on the floor, watching the chain that bounced off the ground between her feet. She could tell they were going to the visitor's area.

Maybe Sean came back, Mary Eileen thought. It had been at least two months since his visit. Mary Eileen had held out hope for at least three weeks that he would return. First, she thought Sean would be back in a week, then two weeks, then a month. Then Mary Eileen decided he was never coming back. But perhaps she'd been wrong. Was Sean waiting for her in the visitor's room? Had he figured out a way, a legal way, to get her out of this place?

Mary Eileen's eyes rose from the floor. Now, she was looking forward to her destination. It must be the visitor's room. It must be Sean. For the first time in two months, Mary Eileen Sullivan smiled.

The guards opened the door and showed Mary Eileen inside where she saw an old man wearing a sports coat and khaki pants, casual yet tailored, and a monogramed blue shirt. Whoever he was, this guy had never seen the inside of the St. Isidore Diner.

"Hello, Mary Eileen," the man said as he rose from the chair on his side of the glass partition. "I am Michael Morris, your new attorney."

Thirty One

Mary Eileen drummed her fingers on the countertop in front of her as she processed the news that she had a new attorney. Doubling her skepticism was the fact that this was coming from the attorney who promised to do his best pro bono. Mary Eileen felt like she was back at work, faced with a coffee bean salesman telling her the price she paid for each bean was going up, and there was nothing she could do to change the future.

She sat back in her chair with an authoritative air that Mary Eileen had not shown in all the days behind bars. In fact, Mary Eileen had lost her alpha attitude the moment Sean and his team had put the handcuffs on her in Detroit. From that time on she stopped being the Mary Eileen who had refused to go back to Ireland after just a taste of America as a foreign exchange student. She no longer was the Mary Eileen who had fought off the advances of one of New York's leading middle-aged, over-sexed chefs; nor was she the Mary Eileen who had found her way to St. Isidore and opened what would become an iconic downtown business.

The Mary Eileen who stood before a judge, and pled guilty to two charges of first-degree murder, was a defeated woman. With head bowed, she mumbled her responses to his questions; and then to those who booked her, stripped her, and humiliated her as she made her entrance to the county jail, and finally, even to her fellow inmates.

But now the old Mary Eileen had returned. She straightened her back, crossed her arms, raised an eyebrow and said, "And why do I need a new attorney?"

"Ms. Sullivan, or may I call you Mary Eileen?"

As Morris received no response except his new client's cold, stony glare, he proceeded to sell himself.

"Ms. Sullivan your public defender isn't much more than a fetus in a pantsuit. She couldn't argue her way out of a traffic ticket."

Mary Eileen sat silently. There was no way a fellow woman be insulted by this misogynist or anyone else unless Mary Eileen was the one doing the insulting.

However, more importantly, she was negotiating. Mary Eileen was always negotiating. It was her drug of choice.

Oh, God, it feels good to be back, she thought.

Still, she didn't faze Morris. He'd met tougher than Mary Eileen Sullivan. Morris had carved a handsome living out of beating murder charges for some of the most heinous criminals in America. He was so good that Morris often didn't even have to go to court. Never without a plea bargain proposition in his back pocket, Morris was more than open to negotiating. He bargained, and he won. That was his drug of choice.

"She let you plead guilty to two murder charges?"

Mary Eileen slowly closed her eyes and nodded in response.

Morris smiled and then furrowed his brow. "That was her first and most fatal mistake," he said. "Never plead guilty to anything, remain innocent until proven guilty. That is my first choice."

Mary Eileen raised an eyebrow. "But I am guilty. I killed those men."

"And that was your first mistake. Not killing, I don't mean that. I am not here to judge," Morris said. "No, your mistake was confessing to the police after they read you your rights."

Mary Eileen slowly leaned forward in her chair, rested her crossed arms on the table and nearly set her pert Irish nose against the glass as she said in her softest, yet most threatening brogue, "So what was my attorney supposed to do?"

"Plead not guilty by reason of insanity."

Mary Eileen jumped to her feet, glanced to her left, saw that the inmate speaking to her attorney two seats down had stopped her conversation, glanced to her right and noticed the guard by the door was reaching for her pepper spray.

Mary Eileen returned to her seat, sat back down, put her hands behind her head and looked at the bright white walls of the visitor's center to calm herself. She had to admire the jail's cleaning staff, yet she also knew why the walls were painted white and not a more soothing color. The strongest bleach in the world could be used to wipe off blood stains, urine, fecal matter, whatever bodily fluids might fly in an argument, without affecting the color of the paint.

"I am not crazy."

"I know you are not. You are not now crazy. But think about this, Ms. Sullivan; would a rational person kill two men, cut up their bodies with a chainsaw, mix cement, stuff the body parts in the cement and hide it all in her cellar? Would a sane person do that?"

Mary Eileen rested her elbows on her knees, looked at the legs of the hideous orange jumpsuit she was forced to wear and the ridiculous wraparound shower shoes all the inmates wore, rested her chin in her hands and touched her lips with her index fingers.

She'd been asking herself the same question. What kind of person would do what I did?

"You are not insane now," Morris continued. "But were you sane when you killed those men? How could this woman I am sitting across from possibly commit such a cold-blooded, calculated act? There is only one explanation. She was temporarily insane. She might need treatment, probably she does. But you, Mary Eileen Sullivan, do not deserve to spend the rest of your life behind bars."

Mary Eileen looked from the table top to Morris' eyes. This new attorney of hers, if he was as good as promised, could not come cheap. Always negotiating, Mary Eileen thought it was time to talk about money.

"I have none."

"Pardon?"

"Money, I have none. They took it all. My bank accounts are in escrow. And since I am guilty, the county or the state or whoever is going to get it all."

"Oh, my Ms. Sullivan," said Morris. "I must apologize. I forgot you've been without the internet or your computers for the last three months. Take a look."

From his briefcase, Morris pulled with a theatrical flourish, an iPad Pro. Being a customer of Verizon Digital, he didn't have to worry about a passcode to get on the jail's wifi system. He quietly opened the pad's cover and turned the screen to face Mary Eileen.

She saw herself. Mary Eileen had become the centerpiece of an online campaign to raise $500,000 to pay for her defense.

"Free Mary Eileen," the banner headline screamed. Tears were in her eyes as Mary Eileen read the paragraphs that described how an abused woman could lose control and kill the men who are keeping her in virtual captivity.

"Mary Eileen Sullivan deserves her day in court..." began one of the graphs.

She didn't read it all. Mary Eileen didn't have to once she saw that the campaign had surpassed its half-million-dollar goal by $250,000.

Suddenly Mary Eileen had three-quarters-of-a-million-dollars pledged to pay for her defense.

Mary Eileen had money and with the cash came power.

She smiled, for the first time, confidently, not submissively. It was time to reinvent herself.

Mary Eileen nodded her head slowly as her eyes rose to meet Morris'.

"But first, a question," Mary Eileen said. "This temporary insanity; where does it go?"

Thirty Two

Mary Eileen made herself as attractive as possible, considering she had to share mirror space with at least a dozen other women and the shower area with even more naked females. But it didn't matter. Her spirit was positively soaring. She would leave at 5 a.m. with a squad of state police troopers for her protection, for Rest Haven, a psychiatric hospital. There, Mary Eileen was going to have the first of three sessions ,agreed to by the court, with Dr. Julianne French.

Mary Eileen was confident Sean would be a part of the state police detachment. He'd promised to stand by her hadn't he? But she was more than a little concerned about Dr. French and the idea that memories hidden would be brought to light.

"This is where we will build our case," Morris had explained in his second meeting with Mary Eileen. "Dr. French is an expert in using hypnotism to release repressed memories."

"And that's a good thing?" Mary Eileen asked.

"Of course it is, Ms. Sullivan. It is how we are going to show that while you are not insane now, or 'crazy' as you put it; you are certainly not responsible for the murders of those men you buried in your cellar."

"I understand. But what if, just for the sake of argument, other memories come up that might include, oh I don't know, some things that I would rather stay, forgotten?"

Morris explained they would deal with that if and when it happened, meaning that he would still be there for her. Why wouldn't he? Knowing that Mary Eileen was cash-flush with seven-hundred-fifty-thousand-dollars and counting for legal expenses, any attorney would be an idiot to dump her by the side of the road.

"Anything else?"

"Yes, just one thing more."

Morris waited. Mary Eileen made sure her thoughts were together before she opened her mouth again.

"One question. If St. Isidore cares so much about me why do I need the state police?"

Morris smiled and nodded. He knew the truth.

"You do have enemies," he said. "There are those who would see you dead. Michigan doesn't have capital punishment. There are some people who are more than willing to be your executioner."

"But this is also part of the show," he continued. "We want to make sure the world is watching."

Mary Eileen knew if she got off, if she was not found guilty, the world would be her oyster.

To her, that made it even more important that she look her best. And Mary Eileen was looking as good as she walked through the county jail to meet the guards for her ride to Rest Haven, and she hoped, Sean.

"Where are the state police?"

"They'll meet us outside."

Mary Eileen moved so quickly the guards had to do a quick skip step to keep up. No longer wearing shower shoes — she'd been given real shoes for her meeting at Rest Haven, along with a gray dress to replace the orange jumpsuit — Mary Eileen felt like her old self.

Her stomach was flipping with excitement, or could it be the baby was moving? It didn't matter to Mary Eileen. Nothing mattered except seeing Sean at the end of the hallway.

The guards tightened their grip on Mary Eileen's arms as they reached a door at the end of the hall. Above it glowed the most beautiful sign Mary Eileen had seen in months: "Exit."

Three black, SUVs waited in the driveway; four state troopers outside each of the vehicles at the front and back of the caravan; two more state cops stood outside the SUV in the middle.

None of them was Sean.

Mary Eileen's enthusiasm that had buoyed her for the past week vanished. Mary Eileen deflated faster than a balloon mistakenly popped by a playful child. It was a good thing the guards had a strong grip. Otherwise, Mary Eileen might have fallen to the pavement.

As her knees faltered, Mary Eileen's head came up; she looked over the hood of the SUV she was to ride in — and saw them.

People were standing elbow-to-elbow and three-deep on the sidewalk across the street. She had not heard them before, but now Mary Eileen couldn't miss the sound. The crowd was cheering! Mostly women and girls from what she could see, but there were some men and boys mixed in; the crowd was chanting her name:

"Free Mary Eileen! Mary Eileen! Free Mary Eileen!"

When the crowd spotted her, a roar of approval replaced the rhythmic chants.

Mary Eileen stood tall. The guards had to push her toward the rear door of the SUV; a state police trooper put his hand on her head to both protect her from the door frame and use his strength to persuade her to get inside.

There was only one way to get to Rest Haven from the jail. It was a short ride. No more than two miles, but the three-vehicle convoy had to thread its way through downtown St. Isidore. The SUVs would have to drive past the Coffee Shoppe.

No one on the sidewalk could see into the SUV thanks to its darkened windows. But Mary Eileen could see that there was never an open space on the sidewalks without people cheering her and waving signs in support of her legal effort. Tears in her eyes fell down her cheeks when her SUV caravan came to a stop because of the crowd that had surged onto DeVos Avenue. People slapped the sides of the SUV, not in a threatening way, but more in a supportive manner. They wanted to let Mary Eileen know they were on her side.

She wished Sean could have seen this.

Two St. Isidore police cars were at the entrance of Rest Haven's parking lot waiting for Mary Eileen. The crowd stayed back to let the SUVs into Rest Haven before walking behind the vehicles and surrounding them as they stopped in front of the hospital's main building.

People were chanting, shouting and applauding as she left the SUV and started walking up the concrete steps of Rest Haven. Mary Eileen made a beautiful impression with a gray skirt with a burgundy top and her auburn hair freshly washed and brushed, tumbling onto her shoulders. With one foot on a step higher than the other and state police troopers on either side of her, Mary Eileen turned to the crowd and smiled.

The resulting roar of approval hit Mary Eileen like one of the straight-line wind storms for which St. Isidore was so famous. The winds seemed like just a breeze for a moment but quickly increased in intensity to reach an almost tornado-like impact before dying to a whisper.

However, this storm of approval and support didn't have a chance to die out. Just as it reached what seemed to be its crescendo, Mary Eileen raised one hand and waved to the crowd. People began to stomp their feet, clap their hands in rhythm and chant her name.

Something inside her told Mary Eileen to start walking before the applause died out. She nearly left the state troopers behind as she turned and strode toward the double-glass doors of Rest Haven. She opened one door, looked back at the crowd, waved again, and blew them a kiss.

As the chanting of her name grew even louder, Mary Eileen walked into Rest Haven's lobby. A tall, confident woman with black hair, streaked with silver drawn up into a bun behind her head was waiting.

She pushed her glasses up on her nose just a bit and smiled down from at least a foot over Mary Eileen's upturned face.

She extended her hand, smiled, and said with a light laugh, "Good morning. You must be Ms. Sullivan. I'm Dr. Julianne French. Are we ready to get started?"

Thirty Three

Patricia Fry watched the Rest Haven demonstration broadcast live on WSIR-TV as she was getting dressed. If her coffee cup had been closer, she would have pitched it at the screen.

"Why are you here?" Jasmine Jameson, WSIR's street reporter, asked a woman in her fifties dressed like she thought she was still in her twenties.

"I've been where Mary Eileen is," the woman replied.

"Under arrest?"

"Oh, God no!" the woman laughed and raised her 'Free Mary Eileen' sign higher as a TV helicopter roared overhead. "I've never been in jail, but I was in relationships that made me feel like I was in prison. Relationships with guys who just wanted a mother, not a real lover."

"Amen, sister," said a woman standing alongside the fifty-something. "These guys, these bastards, need to be taught a lesson."

"Mary Eileen is our hero!" screamed four or five teenage girls, jumping up and down to get on camera.

"We're going out to the banks of the Red Run River," Jasmine said while being jostled by people trying to get their fifteen-seconds of fame on WSIR. "Jason Harley is on the river bank, right in the middle of another demonstration showing support for Mary Eileen Sullivan."

"Thanks, Jasmine," Jason said as his face appeared on Patricia's TV screen further unsettling the coffee sloshing in her stomach.

"Oh for Christ's sake," she muttered. Patricia was no longer sitting in her breakfast nook enjoying a bagel with cream cheese. Now she was pacing. And she was getting close to that coffee cup that could become a missile at any moment.

"I am surrounded by a crowd of teenagers who have rallied on th banks of the Red Run River rather than going to class today..."

"Oh that's a surprise," Patricia said to her TV screen.

The camera panned back to show a rather small crowd of hig school kids, none of whom gave any confidence to Baby Boomers wh were wondering who would be running the USA in another ten c twenty years.

But it must have made the owner of Retro Plus in downtown S Isidore, where one could always find a torn Led Zeppelin t-shirt, ecst tic.

As soon as the WSIR producer in the remote broadcasting truc realized the camera had panned back too far and viewers at home coul see there were only five or six kids, nothing even close to a "crowd c teenagers," she ordered a closeup of Jason and his first interview.

"She is the 'Murder Babe,'" the teenager screamed into Jason's m crophone.

"Fuck right," shouted the only two kids behind him who were pay ing attention.

"I'm sorry, what? The Murder Babe?"

"Yeah, she is so fucking hot! Love ya, Mary Eileen Sullivan!"

Clinging to whatever shreds of decency were left, the chief produ er at the WSIR studio switched back to a shot of the crowd outsid Rest Haven. There, the camera, unfortunately, discovered several sigr reading, 'Mary Eileen — the Murder Babe,' and 'We Love the Murd Babe,' had appeared, along with several women who had ripped o their shirts when they spotted the red "on air' light glowing on the cam era.

The producer quickly went from that camera, leaving Jasmin gulping like a fish out of water, in mid-sentence, and switched to a vie of the steps of Rest Haven just as Mary Eileen turned from the doubl glass doors, waved and then blew a kiss to the crowd.

The VU meter that was registering the crowd noise being broadcast by WSIR pegged in the red; its needle buried to the right, as a volcano of emotional support erupted from the hundreds of people standing in front of Rest Haven and across the street.

"Michael Morris, that fucker," Patricia muttered to herself as she stabbed the 'off' button on her remote control. "He must have staged this rally, this 'spontaneous show of support,'" Patricia said as she did air quotes with her fingers.

To punctuate her mood, she tossed the coffee cup into the metal kitchen sink, enjoyed the clang of ceramic on metal, and looked around her small, one-bedroom apartment. It was the best she could afford in downtown St. Isidore. "But if I fuck this up, I'll be stuck in some little country courthouse living over a grocery store," she muttered again.

Well, that wasn't going to happen. Patricia made up her mind that not only would this case cement her position in the St. Isidore County Prosecutor's Office, but it would also be one giant step in this woman's quest to make it to the State Capitol Building and maybe even Washington.

But first, she had to lock up Mary Eileen Sullivan on two charges of murder. Life without parole — the people, would accept nothing less, Patricia decided.

Now she just needed to find twelve men and women who would agree.

"When it's a challenge to seat an impartial jury in a murder case it is usually because most people have their minds made up — the accused is guilty and needs to hang, or whatever," Fry said later in the day to her staff.

"But this case is going to be different. Thanks to social media and a well-constructed campaign by her defense attorney, Michael Morris; there is strong support for Mary Eileen Sullivan to be declared not guilty because of insanity, or God forbid; innocent."

"We are not going to let that happen."

Patricia had already written assignments for each member of her twelve-person team on three whiteboards in the conference room. At first, she'd been expected —and had been planning to run this case alone, maybe with a second at the prosecution table, but no one besides a two-person team. However, the strength of the Mary Sullivan for Sainthood social media campaign had led her to ask for help and persuaded her boss to grant the request.

The dozen people on the team would now fan out into St. Isidore, digging into the histories of the men whose body parts had been found hidden in the cellar under the Coffee Shoppe. Patricia would spend her time — just as Dr. Julianne French was doing — finding out everything she could about Mary Eileen Sullivan.

"And, I will tell you something else, we are going to get our fucking county psychiatrist on the case."

Thirty Four

To say Mary Eileen had drawn up her castle's bridge so she could stop everyone from crossing her psychological moat would be an understatement. There was just no way she wanted this Dr. French to be picking around inside her brain, unlocking her emotions, discovering her deepest, darkest secrets.

Sean's the only one who has the right to do that, she thought. And he can only do it because I allow it.

Sean was the guy who had permission, but he blew it. Mary Eileen hadn't seen or heard from him in months. So that bridge to her psyche was pretty much burned. And it hurt.

Does this Dr. French think I am going to let her into my mind?

Even the Rest Haven building put Mary Eileen on edge. The doors whispered open and closed. Everything smelled new. The furniture in Dr. French's office looked like it was never used more than once, almost like she exchanged it for new after every patient. When Mary Eileen had followed Dr. French to her office, everyone else —and they were all wearing bright white doctor coats — was walking on eggshells up and down the hallways. It was almost like they were afraid of rattling the psychiatric patients. Rest Haven was a nuthouse. Mary Eileen had to remember that, and she was one of the nuts — cashews preferably, pronouncing it cash-EWS in her mind just like in her homeland across the Atlantic.

That was another problem. Thinking of herself as crazy was something Mary Eileen had contemplated for years. But she had finally rejected it only because there was no time to be nuts. She had to earn a living.

That's probably something the esteemed Dr. French has never had to do, Mary Eileen thought. Diplomas on the wall showed Dr. French had done her undergraduate work at Yale, then went to Harvard Medical School. God, she must be so stuck up, Mary Eileen thought. Just like most of my customers.

The view was spectacular, or as grand as it could be in St. Isidore. Dr. French's floor-to-ceiling window that ran the length of the longest wall looked out over the Red Run River — the good part of the river. No ratty teenagers smoking dope on the banks here, no, Mary Eileen thought, only the right people were on the water in this part of town. Everyone was driving the latest Subaru or Volvo, topped with kayaks, filled with beautiful children, dogs, and wives.

"I'll bet they never had to step over a drunk to get into their office," Mary Eileen muttered.

"Pardon me," Dr. French said, just loud enough to break Mary Eileen out of her daydream.

It didn't take a Harvard Medical School graduate, top of her class no less, to see there was a psychological problem that was crippling Mary Eileen. Her hands were so twisted that Dr. French winced. Mary Eileen was grinding her teeth that weren't chewing her lower lip, as she looked out the window, and a vein was pulsing on her right temple.

"Shall we begin?"

Mary Eileen whipped her head around so fast that a new doctor would have brought her hands up into a defensive fighting position. With her Taekwondo training, Dr. French was more than qualified to fight back if it got physical, but she wasn't worried about Mary Eileen. But then again, maybe that was a mistake. After all, she was confronting a woman charged with killing two men.

"Let's sit over here."

At least I don't have to do that cliche thing of laying down on a shrink's couch, Mary Eileen thought. But when she sat in the overstuffed chair opposite Dr. French, her guard remained in place.

"I imagine you have been wondering about 'repressed memories,'" Dr. French said with a smile and air quotes.

"Actually, no, I have not," Mary Eileen might have said if she had felt like speaking. She would have added, "I have not been wondering about 'repressed memories,'" making her air quotes as sarcastic as possible, "because I think this is all bullshit, and I believe you are so full of it that your blue eyes are turning brown."

Instead, of saying any of that, Mary Eileen crossed her arms in front of her. This conversation with Dr. French was no different from a discussion with a coffee bean salesman, no different at all.

The smile never left Dr. French's face. Just like a salesman.

She leaned forward in the overstuffed chair opposite Mary Eileen and rested her elbows on her knees as the look on her face slowly evolved from one showing smiling acceptance to an attitude of concern. She paused before saying, "I am not sure yet if your problem is with repressed memories or if you fear what we might discover. Let me begin by talking about what repressed memories are, so that is no confusion going forward."

Mary Eileen sighed, looked at the ceiling, and crossed her arms tighter.

Dr. French settled back into her chair. Patients who were most troubled by repressed memories often took the same attitude being displayed by Mary Eileen.

"Doctors, like myself, have known for years that our patients were hiding memories from themselves, but it was confirmed recently by a Northwestern University study," she said.

"Those memories are often hidden to protect you from emotional pain triggered by recalling the event. In a way that's good, because your mind is protecting you from yourself. But Northwestern found if the memories are locked up, bottled up in your psyche for too long; serious problems, psychological problems, can result."

Mary Eileen had slowly returned her gaze from the ceiling to Dr. French.

"So, how do we do that? How do we release these memories?"

A positive sign, Dr. French thought. Questions are always an indication that the patient might be willing to cooperate and assist in her recovery. Without that, all of Dr. French's years of education and professional experience added up to nothing.

"We have to return the brain to the same state of consciousness it was in when your brain created or encoded the memories."

Mary Eileen turned the palms of her hands up, lifted an eyebrow, tilted her head to the left briefly and said, "How?"

"We could use drugs. There are two amino acids, glutamate, and GABA, that are the yin and yang of the brain. These acids direct our emotional tides. They control whether nerve cells are excited, calm, or inhibited," Dr. French said. She was getting excited now, just as a used car salesman feels when he senses the customer is ready to press hard to sign three copies of a contract.

"Gaboxadol is one drug that has worked. It stimulates the GABA receptors."

Mary Eileen's eyes clouded a bit, and she tensed at the thought of losing control to drugs.

"And, we know this, how?"

"Experiments on mice have shown us..."

Dr. French could almost hear Mary Eileen's eyeballs rolling in her head. Mary Eileen leaned back in her chair, laughed, smiled and said, "You are kidding, I hope. Has it ever worked on people?"

"But I dislike drugs. There is another option."

Why do I need this? Mary Eileen thought. This town loves me. Did you see all of those people out there? What jury in its right mind is going to send me to prison?

It hadn't occurred to her until her caravan — and Mary Eileen was thinking of it as 'her caravan' — but people loved her and loved her story. She could see herself talking to Oprah, Matt Lauer on the "Today" show and George Stephanopoulos on "Good Morning America."

Who needs his stuck-up bimbo, Dr. French? Mary Eileen was pushing herself up and out of the chair when her better judgment took over. If she left now, the two state police troopers guarding the door in the hallway would take her right back to jail. So, she stayed. Let Dr. French talk, Mary Eileen decided. It will just be another chapter in my book.

Instead of leaving, Mary Eileen sat back down and tried to look like she was paying attention. But she was thinking about her book, TV interviews and selling the movie rights to her story. Good God, Mary Eileen thought. The best days are ahead of me. I just have to reinvent myself one more time.

Thirty Five

Mary Eileen Sullivan would be Michael Morris' ticket to the big time. He envisioned appearing on CNN, MSNBC, maybe even ABC, CBS and NBC to discuss the case, his client, and how he saved her from a life behind bars. However, the report from Dr. French's first session with Mary Eileen was pushing those dreams closer to the trash can.

Morris punched his foot down on the accelerator of his new BMW Alpina B6 Gran Coupe to ease the pain. He was cruising US-131 north of St. Isidore, just driving. The four-lane freeway was a straight line all the way to Cadillac. Nothing to think about except how to win this case. There had to be a way.

Michael Morris had started life in 1955 as the son of a teacher and a librarian. His mom had left the Detroit Public Library system when he was born. She would be a full-time mother. That's what women did back in the day. His dad pulled the family out of the Motor City and moved to the suburbs. That's what white families did back in the day. The Morris family wasn't wealthy, but they didn't miss any meals either. At the end of two decades, there was enough money left over to send Michael to college.

However, that life wasn't enough for Michael Morris. He realized he needed more when he met Sheila Watson as an undergrad at the University of Michigan. Morris grew up in Warren, a blue-collar suburb built by GM. Sheila was from Birmingham, Michigan, surrounded by the families that made GM.

She was not only the spark that lit Morris' sexual drive; Sheila Watson was the motivation for Morris to become rich enough to pay cash for his $122,000 BMW. But there was more. Her family laughed at Michael. Sheila dumped Michael. He vowed she'd be the last bitch to ever to that to him. And nobody would ever laugh again.

Now, Morris had money. He was well-known. But Michael wanted more. He wanted to be powerful. Being an attorney was just a step in that direction.

This Mary Eileen Sullivan case could get him there. But what looked like a slam dunk a month ago was now appearing to be a nightmare of career calamity.

Just as Morris was coping with the reality that he might just be defending a mass murderer who knew what she was doing; his smartphone rang. It was his mysterious benefactor, the man who orchestrated an incredible social media campaign that included Facebook, Twitter, and Kickstarter. It was a campaign that raised more than three-quarters-of-a-million-dollars.

When Morris saw the benefactor's number come up on his iPhone screen, he nearly sent the call to voice mail.

Against his better judgment, Morris answered the call.

"Have you seen French's report?"

"Yes, of course, I have."

"Do we have any defense left?"

Why did I answer this phone? Morris wondered. Suddenly I am on the losing end of a trial the country and maybe around the world, will be watching, and I am going to get creamed.

"A verdict of not guilty because of insanity will be tough to win. But there is still hope."

"Hope? Are you kidding? This report shows Mary Eileen created some female superhero character for herself, but in actuality, she was pretty much a slut who had been flitting from man to man and may have killed others when she was disappointed."

"I can read," Morris muttered.

"Pardon me?"

"Sorry, I did read that. But I think the superhero angle might b just what we need. She thought she was something of avenging ange right?"

"She has been searching for a man to replace her father who she be lieves was killed by a British commando unit fighting the IRA but wa most probably murdered by her alcoholic mother," said the voice on th phone.

"Yes, and there is our hope, and no I am not kidding," Morris said

"We can still win this case and keep Mary Eileen out of prison. Bu we are going to have to invest more money in the defense. I want t bring an expert criminologist in on the case. The person I am thinkin of has a history of examining first-time offenders, people who migh have committed crimes, but had no understanding of the conse quences."

"More money? How much more?"

Morris paused. He didn't want to jump too fast. Being able to ge another quarter-million-dollars would take lots of finesse.

"We are looking at another three-hundred to maybe four-hundred thousand dollars."

"Jesus Christ."

"Oh but this money would be well spent..."

"Just like the last $750,000 we raised and you spent?"

"We can't stop now," Morris said. It was time to play his hole car "If we surrender, Mary Eileen Sullivan is doomed."

No response came from the man who evidently cared more abo Mary Eileen Sullivan than anything else in the world. He told Morr his only motivation was to spare a woman he considered innocent, b Morris had a feeling there was more to his story. Not that it mattere All Morris wanted was a win. A victory would cement his position o the top shelf of the nation's attorneys. If he lost, no one would ever he from him again.

And, Morris was afraid that if he didn't get out of the country fast, and to the little island chain where he had deposited about a quarter-million of the money raised for Ms. Sullivan's defense, he would never get a second chance.

"I know we are running low on money, but let's make another push on Facebook, or maybe a new Kickstarter campaign."

"Not a chance of that, I'm afraid."

Morris was silent. He had to agree. Both of the men knew that America's love for Mary Eileen Sullivan had faded. She was no longer the "Murder Babe" idolized by cable TV show hosts for the ratings she brought to their shows. No longer did every legal pundit in the U.S. point to her case as the work of misogynistic men.

Her flame was flickering out as a wave of copycat killers; teenage girls who began killing their boyfriends, male school teachers and even their fathers, swept the nation. The simple act of murder wasn't enough for some of these children. Several of the girls had persuaded their boyfriends to commit suicide.

America's cable TV shows were at once shocked and revolted. Mary Eileen was no longer a hero. Now she was a villain.

"The best Kickstarter campaign in the world won't raise the money we need," the mysterious man on the phone told Morris.

The ringtone from his second phone saved Morris from saying again it was time to fish or cut bait. It was Michael's secretary on Face Time. Morris punched up the call on his dashboard WiFi. Teri was the latest in a series of college undergrads who were lured to work for him at minimum wage with a promise of an excellent resume reference and free pot. The company car, a "previously owned" BMW that she was allowed to use didn't hurt either.

His body temperature went from 98.6 to somewhere in the Arctic Circle range when Teri held up a manila envelope. On it was stamped the St. Isidore County Prosecutor's seal.

"Hang on a minute. Fry just sent me something," Morris told the man on the first phone as he put his first smartphone on hold.

"Open it," he told Teri. "Let me see what's inside."

After a couple of seconds of watching Teri wrestling to get the envelope open, Morris' face turned the color of vanilla ice cream. He thanked Teri and went back to his first smartphone.

"Fry's motioning for a court-appointed psychiatrist to examine Mary Eileen," Morris told his money man. "Now it's all going to come out."

Thirty Six

Patricia was in her element as she presented her case against Mary Eileen, who stoically listened to the testimony. The jury was hers. Spotting the flop sweat stains on Michael Morris' stiff shirt collar was a bonus.

Patricia could have been standing in a refrigerated box car as she adroitly wove a tale of a woman who was willing to kill until she got what she wanted; using the testimony of fifty witnesses and seven experts, the best of whom was the county psychiatrist, Dr. Hank Kastle.

Patricia said Mary Eileen was a manipulative liar who was prepared to do anything to her advantage. In her opening statement, Patricia called her a "singularly cold-blooded and unscrupulous killer."

Patricia encouraged the jury to look beyond the composed, attractive woman seated at the defendant's table, to see the evil in her heart.

But here was the prosecution's problem: evidence showed Mary Eileen was not on the same planet most people when it came to ethical decisions. Even though she was a defense witness, Dr. Julianne French admitted Mary Eileen was a "user of men" and a borderline nymphomaniac. However, Dr. French stressed it was those personality traits that made it difficult for Mary Eileen to keep more than a tenuous grip on reality.

"She grew up believing that her father was murdered in Ireland by British soldiers because of his IRA connections. Her father was her hero. After his death, she began a search for a replacement," Dr. French testified.

"Replacement?" Morris asked.

"Yes, absolutely," Dr. French responded. "Mary Eileen Sullivan was like a princess who just wanted to be rescued by a man. Each of her affairs were a step in that quest. Each man she loved or thought she loved, for a time, offered a slice of her father's personality. But she was never able to find one man as good as her father, until..."

"Until?"

Dr. French paused. She licked her lips and looked at the defendant's table.

"Mary Eileen Sullivan is pregnant."

Judge Leopold and the jury snapped to attention. Patricia Fry could just imagine the people of the world, watching on CNN, the BBC, and just about every other cable channel on Earth leaning toward their television sets.

"Who is the father? Do we know?" Morris asked.

"Yes, I believe we do."

"Is Mary Eileen Sullivan accused of killing the father of her as-yet-unborn child?"

"No," answered Dr. French. "The father of her child is undoubtedly the only man who could come close to filling the emptiness left by her father's death."

"Is the father of her child in this courtroom?"

Dr. French paused and looked over the audience. Spectators and reporters jammed the courtroom. There was hardly enough air to breathe. And Dr. French's blockbuster revelation had just sucked what little oxygen there was to spare out of the room.

"I wouldn't know," said Dr. French. "Mary Eileen Sullivan refused to tell me."

"Does she know?"

"Yes, I believe she does."

"But no matter who the father may be," Morris said as Patricia flinched. Here it comes, she thought; he's pushing the sympathy button.

"No matter who the father is," Morris continued, "Mary Eileen Sullivan will have her baby in prison if convicted, and will never have a chance to raise the child as her own."

"Objection!" Patricia shouted. "That is not germane to this case. Whether or not the defendant is allowed to raise her child is irrelevant. The question at hand is whether she knowingly murdered two men and then callously disposed of their bodies."

"Sustained," Judge Leopold said. "The jury and witness will disregard the last question from Mr. Morris."

Patricia may have won that point, but to take set and match, she was going to have to move the jury back to making a factually based decision rather than one based on emotion. She always knew that is what would make the difference between victory and defeat.

"Mary Eileen Sullivan is a sympathetic person," Patricia told her roommate Allyson more than once. "She's attractive, intelligent, speaks several languages, and owned a business in town. There are not many people in St. Isidore who haven't purchased a coffee and scone from her."

"Even if she's a killer?" Allyson said.

"Yeah," Patricia said as she leaned back from the oak desk that had become the centerpiece of her home life with Allyson. "Even if she's a killer."

"But why? Why would any jury decide to let her free?"

"Because in their hearts, they want her to be innocent."

Patricia decided not to cross examine Dr. French. She didn't want to get into a battle of words over whether repressed memories were valid. Dr. French was the expert. She had the diplomas, Patricia's law degree, even though it came from the University of Michigan, would be no match. And just as Patricia realized the jury might want Mary Eileen Sullivan to be innocent; they also wanted to believe Dr. Julianne French.

Patricia called Dr. Hank Kastle to the stand.

Henry "Hank" Kastle was a first-generation American. His parents, who escaped from East Germany just as the Soviets were building the Berlin Wall, called him "Hank" rather than his given name. "It sounds so much more American," his mother said to her fellow German immigrant neighbors.

"Tell me, Dr. Kastle, we heard much about the alleged 'repressed memories' of Mary Eileen Sullivan. As a graduate of the Harvard Medical School, who has his doctorate in psychiatric medicine, what has your experience been with 'repressed memories?'" Patricia said after Hank had sworn to tell the truth and nothing but the truth.

Even though Dr. Kastle was only 5-foot, 8-inches tall and could not have weighed more than 150 pounds, he was a charismatic if not imposing figure in the witness stand. As he swung his gaze to the jury box, not one of the six men and six women were able to drop their eyes from his.

Hank shifted his attention back to Patrica and said with a smile between his salt-and-pepper mustache and goatee, "There should be a label attached to any and all repressed memory cases; 'Warning: The concept of repressed memory has not been validated with experimental research. Its use may be hazardous to accurate interpretation of clinical behavior.'"

"Objection," shouted Morris from the defendant's table.

"Overruled," said Judge Leopold.

Patricia returned Hank's smile.

"Dr. Kastle, you interviewed the defendant, Mary Eileen Sullivan, for more than thirty hours. Were you able to find any psychological problems associated with her childhood any evidence of repressed memories?"

Hank leaned forward, put his elbows on the edge of the witness stand, formed a triangle with his fingers and looked at Mary Eileen. When he answered, Hank was speaking to her as much as he was addressing Patricia, Judge Leopold, and the jury.

Hank said, "There is no question that Mary Eileen Sullivan, the defendant, does not see the world in the same way as you or me."

Morris was stunned, as was the jury and even Judge Leopold. The prosecution's chief witness, the star that Patricia Fry had held close to her chest until today had agreed with the defense. Was Mary Eileen Sullivan not a rational person?

It was only their fear they would miss something, even more, headline-worthy that kept the media from leaping out of their chairs and dashing out to use their phones in the hallway.

Judge Leopold's eyebrows nearly danced off her face until she noticed Patricia was still smiling.

"Well, let me rephrase if I may," Hank continued. "She sees the same information we see, but her mind processes it differently and comes to a different conclusion."

"Do you mean she is, insane?"

"I didn't say that. Mary Eileen Sullivan, I believe, has a grave, comprehensive, multi-faceted personality disorder. But she is not insane."

"Do you mean she knows the difference between right and wrong?"

"Absolutely, yes, Mary Eileen Sullivan knows the difference."

"And no matter what effect her repressed memories may or may not have had; did she then, and does she now realize it was wrong to kill two men, cut up their corpses with a chain saw and hide their body parts beneath the Coffee Shoppe?"

The jury, Judge Leopold, and Michael Morris stopped breathing. Hank took his time, looking from the jury box to his left, sweeping his gaze across the defendant's table and up to Judge Leopold on his right before he said, "Yes, she did. She realized that killing those men and disposing of the bodies to cover up the crime was wrong. Mary Eileen Sullivan knew it was wrong then. She knows it now."

"Was she responsible for her actions?"

Hank rested his chin in his hands, looked down, closed his eyes, took a breath and looked up.

“Yes.”

As he looked at Mary Eileen Sullivan, Hank continued, “She was responsible then, and she is now.”

“Was the defendant trying to ‘replace her father,’ as Dr. Julianne French has suggested?”

“I believe not.”

“What if anything does her father and Mary Eileen Sullivan’s memory have to do with this case?”

“I believe the defendant was not trying to ‘replace her father’ by dating, sleeping with and even marrying men before murdering them.”

Patricia said not a word. She crossed her arms and stepped back so Hank had a direct line of sight to the jury box.

“I believe that psychologically she was trying to kill her father.”

The courtroom exploded in furious emotion. Reporters were rushing to the hallway; some people were standing and cheering, others were in tears. Judge Leopold nearly broke her gavel pounding it on her desk to demand quiet.

When the chaos finally settled, Judge Leopold looked to Patricia.

“I rest my case,” A.P. Fry said.

“Do you have anything further?” Judge Leopold said to Michael Morris.

“Yes, your honor, a final witness."

"And who might that be?"

"Mary Eileen Sullivan."

A second blast of emotional sound and fury had to be gaveled down by Judge Leopold.

"There will be silence in this courtroom!” she said as the sound of her wooden gavel against her antique oak desk competed with the babble of conversation, sobbing, and sounds of outrage.

Leopold stood and swung the gavel from her shoulder to the desk until all in the room were silent and seated.

Judge Leopold let the silence hang as thick as the humidity on an August afternoon and then said quietly, "We are recessed until 9 o'clock tomorrow."

Thirty Seven

Nearly one-hundred people filed into a courtroom built for eighty-five, one by one, after first passing through two metal detection posts and then a court deputy with a wand. The crowd was much more subdued than the previous day's audience. Gone was the carnival atmosphere of people looking for a vicarious thrill. There was no easy banter nor friendly verbal jousting. And for the first time in forever, it was even difficult to lay a bet down on the verdict in Mary Eileen Sullivan's trial.

"What do you think, Tony?" Julie had asked yesterday as her eyes flickered with excitement. The past three days had been better than TV, "Does she get off?"

"Yeah, I think so," said Tony who was much more interested in what he perceived as his destiny with Julie than Mary Eileen's fate. Both were huge fans of true crime television shows and documentaries. He and Julie had set up tents on opposite sides of the courthouse lawn two days before Mary Eileen's trial began. Retired, after twenty-five years toiling at St. Isidore Foundry, they were ready to relax. Unfortunately, relaxation became boredom, so separately, they had decided to move away from their TV sets and get a taste of real life.

Gradually their tents had moved closer together until finally there was no need for two anymore.

The day before they'd been lighthearted and excited. Today, Tony and Julie were almost somber as they prepared to hear from the killer herself.

Others of retirement age with the freedom to hang out at St. Isidore's trial of the century went entrepreneurial. Suzie and Joseph had been selling homemade hangman's noose-and-tree ceramic figurines to the Deadies who came from around the world to visit St. Isidore's Suicide Forest. After first selling their little statues of men, women, children, and families swinging from trees, from a roadside cart, Suzie and Joseph had rented a storefront on DeVos Avenue. Business boomed. They opened a second location. But sensing the aroma of fresh opportunity and money, the couple had pulled their cart out of the barn on their twenty-acre hobby farm — purchased with their business profits, thank you Deadies very much — and set up shop on the courthouse lawn.

Adam King, who owned the Reading Room, St. Isidore's premier (and only) bookstore, moved racks of true crime books to the sidewalk outside the courthouse. He knew a business opportunity when he saw one. Adam wasn't alone. St. Isidore's tavern and restaurant owners opened an impromptu food festival the week of Mary Eileen's trial.

Of course, what little criminal underworld there was in St. Isidore also sensed a chance to make money off the trial. Bookies had been taking bets for months on the fate of Mary Eileen.

But today, the audience, many of whom had lined up outside the courthouse before sunrise, knew that they would be witness to a historic day and were treating it with the reverence they felt the moment deserved.

Once the crowd was settled, and Judge Leopold in her seat, the first and only witness of the day was called to the stand; Mary Eileen Sullivan.

"You swear to tell the truth, the whole truth, so help you, God?"

"I do."

Late night TV show comics had made more than a few jokes about what would happen when Mary Eileen's hand touched the Bible.

The fire-and-brimstone crowd was disappointed, of course. Mary Eileen's hand came away unscathed.

Instead of crying out in agony, she and her audience settled in for what all knew could be an emotional confrontation when it was Patrica Fry's turn to cross-examine.

Michael Morris approached his client.

"Why did you decide to take the stand? I never let my clients do this unless I am sure they are innocent. You insisted, and I relented. I am not certain this is in your best interest, yet you do. Why?" Morris asked.

Mary Eileen paused and looked down as she touched the small silver cross on her necklace. It was the only piece of jewelry she wore, so it stood out against the dark gray dress she had worn through her trial.

Just as Judge Leopold opened her mouth to prod Mary Eileen to answer the question, she spoke.

"I want to tell my story without psychiatrists or anyone else getting in the way."

All twelve members of the jury, as did the audience, leaned forward, some nearly falling out of their chairs to make sure they didn't miss a word. Reporters stopped scribbling. There would be no need for notes. All felt that the words they were about to hear would remain ingrained in their memories for all time.

"Fine, let's begin. Mary Eileen, did you kill David Van Holt?"

Her eyes grew shiny with tears as Mary Eileen looked into her attorney's eyes and then at the jury, before glancing back down at her hands.

"Mary Eileen..." Morris prodded his client. Testifying and subjecting herself to cross-examination had been all Mary Eileen's idea. But as they discussed the testimony the night before, Morris began to think this might be the best way to persuade a judge and jury to send his client to a mental health facility for treatment, rather than being warehoused in prison.

And from a purely selfish point of view, Morris knew the world was seeing this trial on cable TV and was no less interested than any of the people in the courtroom. That couldn't be anything but good for him, as long as Morris was able to make Mary Eileen lose control. He wanted her to lose it, emotionally, but not so much that the jury became afraid of her. He wanted their sympathy, not their fear, or worse, their revulsion.

Before she sat down in the witness booth, it had been a long night for Mary Eileen. Talking to Morris and being forced to relive the nightmares of two murders, and the bloody cover up of both killings had been horrendous for Mary Eileen. She had been obliged to bring up everything she'd kept hidden from the world, even from herself. Mary Eileen had thrashed about in the orange plastic chair. She had slammed first her fists, then her head on the table between her and Morris.

This morning, Mary Eileen looked back up at Morris, took a breath, and whispered, "Yes, yes, I did it."

"You did what?"

Mary Eileen paused again.

"Mary Eileen, what did you do to David Van Holt?"

"I killed him."

"Louder please."

"I killed him!" Mary Eileen nearly stood up but caught herself as a court bailiff was moving to her side to push her back down into her seat.

"I killed him," she whispered, slumping in the hard wooden chair.

Morris said as gently as possible, "How did you take the life of David Van Holt?"

Mary Eileen was distracted by the sound of David's mother gently weeping.

Judge Leopold looked up but decided not to use her gavel. After suffering two miscarriages, she understood only too well a mother's grief.

"I shot him in the head. I came up behind him with my gun, and I shot him in the head."

"Oh my God!" said David's mother from the third row.

Two men helped her out of the courtroom.

Michael Morris paused. He licked his lips and looked at the jury trying to gauge how they were taking his client's admission. Surprisingly, they seemed concerned for Mary Eileen Sullivan.

As Morris looked back at his client, he realized why. Mary Eileen's expression had changed. Her chin was thrust out. Her shoulders were straight. She was no long slumped in the chair.

Morris asked,"Why?"

"He would not leave my apartment. We were divorced. I told him to leave. He would not. What was I supposed to do? I had a life to live," Mary Eileen said as she slapped her hands on the oak railing in front of her. "I have a life to live! Damn it! He had no right!"

"So, you shot him?"

"Yes."

"Tell me more about how and why it happened."

Mary Eileen began to tremble, just as she had in the jail's visitor's room the night before. Morris had her very, very close to the edge. Mary Eileen hesitated. She chewed her lip. Morris didn't push. He waited.

"I didn't remember any of it, until my first session with Dr. French. But now I do. I remember the bullets hitting his head, and it was like his face exploded. He fell on to the table. And David was gone."

Mary Eileen's stern facade had faded. Now she was an attractive young woman whose auburn hair was all the more stunning because of her pale complexion.

"But until your sessions with Dr. French, you did not remember the actual murder?"

"No, I did not."

"Did you, or do you, remember cutting up his body with a chain saw, putting it in cement and hiding the body parts in your cellar?"

"I do now."

"Does this seem a rational act to you?"

"Objection," Patricia Fry said. "He's asking the witness to reach a conclusion that she is not qualified to make."

"Overruled," said Judge Leopold. She and the world wanted to hear Mary Eileen's answer.

Thirty Eight

Sally Randall, the jury foreperson, felt crushed by her responsibility. Not only was it up to her to lead the other eleven members of the jury to an unanimous decision; she, as did the other jurors, had the responsibility of deciding if a young woman should spend the rest of her life behind bars.

Was this an unbiased jury? Sally didn't believe so, and neither, if they were honest, did her colleagues in the jury box. How could anyone in St. Isidore not have heard of the murders of these two men? Even if they hadn't, how could any person who worked within two miles of the Coffee Shoppe not have purchased a coffee or a bagel from Mary Eileen Sullivan?

Judge Leopold, who was the kind of woman Sally dreamed her daughters would become, said the jurors only needed to be able to say that they had not made up their mind about the case.

Sally couldn't speak for the rest of the jury's honesty, but she had not decided if Mary Eileen should be found not guilty because of insanity.

Michael Morris explained to the jury in his opening statement the difference between a defendant being "not guilty" or "innocent."

"'Not guilty' is a legal term," Morris had said. "It means that under the law as you understand it when you reach your decision, Mary Eileen Sullivan was 'not guilty' because she was legally insane at the time of the killings. If you find her to be 'not guilty,' you will not be declaring that she is 'innocent.'"

Morris paused to let the concept sink in. Not only was he legally accurate, but Morris could also see that in one paragraph, he had relieved much of the burden that weighed down on the jurors, at least those who cared about reaching a fair and honest verdict.

"Let me be the first, and I dare say I will not be the last, to tell you that Mary Eileen Sullivan did kill David Van Holt and Hans Mueller. She shot both of these men, ended their lives far too early, then proceeded to cut up their bodies with a chain saw and bury them with cement in the cellar of the Coffee Shoppe."

Again, Morris paused if only to see the reaction of his jury. And, at that moment, the jury was his. Morris wore his most expensive suits in the courtroom. But, it wouldn't have mattered if he had worn jeans. When it came to captivating a jury, Michael Morris was a force of nature.

"The attorney, especially defense lawyers in murder trials, is on a pedestal in the eyes of jurors," Morris told a table of second-year law students assembled in his office for coffee, scones, and wisdom. "These poor folks have never cracked a law book. They have never before come close to a courtroom or even had an encounter on the wrong side of the law with a police officer. They could not be more in awe of their surroundings than if they had somehow landed next to a surgeon performing a heart transplant."

"Sadly, most of my fellow defense attorneys, as will most of you I fear, either forget or never understand that fact of life," Morris said. "Most lawyers don't talk down to a jury, as they should; they try to be on the same level with the jurors. The jury doesn't need that anymore than a dog needs to take its owner for a walk."

Indeed, Sally and the rest of the jury felt beholden to Morris for doing them the favor of walking them through the explanation of the difference between 'innocent' and 'not guilty.'

"So, Mary Eileen Sullivan is not innocent," continued Morris to the jury. "But I would argue that she is most definitely not guilty by reason of temporary insanity. After all, how many of us have considered killing a neighbor, a co-worker, or even a spouse."

Now, he paused to smile at the jurors, and they returned his grin. They were in on the joke. All twelve felt they were partners with Morris.

With a smile, he added, "But how many of us have pulled the trigger, or plunged the blade of a knife into the object of our anger?"

With the rhetorical question hanging in the air, Morris waited again, to give the jurors a chance to look at each other and smile.

"None of us have," Morris said, and after a beat pause, added, "right?"

Several jurors looked at each other and chuckled.

"And why not?" Morris asked. "Because we knew it would be the wrong thing to do, or we knew we would be punished if caught; or perhaps, no matter how angry we got, we knew the difference between right and wrong."

The jury nodded its agreement as one.

"Ladies and gentlemen of the jury, I implore you to give me the opportunity to show you that Mary Eileen Sullivan is not innocent; she did kill two men. But that sense of reason you all possess that keeps you from sitting where she is now," and he swept his hand through the air, directing the jury's eyes to the defendant's table, "is that same sense of reason that Mary Eileen Sullivan somehow lost, in what was, I contend, a moment of temporary insanity."

Sally Randall didn't remember a word of Patrica Fry's opening statement. But she could have recited Michael Morris' speech in her sleep. In fact, it had not been a speech, Morris was speaking directly to her, Sally was sure of that.

Sally had been angry enough at her ex-husband to kill him. She had not, but even today, twenty years after the divorce, there were nights Sally dreamed of his assassination. Sally felt that she understood where Mary Eileen was the minute before she pulled the trigger of the gun that killed David Van Holt and Hans Mueller. But, for some reason, while Sally was able to turn the heat down on the burner of her anger; Mary Eileen Sullivan was not.

Sally wanted to know why Mary Eileen had killed, perhaps to answer the question of why she had not.

So, like Judge Leopold and the rest of the world; Sally Randall, and her eleven peers waited for Mary Eileen's response.

Thirty Nine

Patricia Fry knew her career was sitting on the witness stand. That wasn't Mary Eileen Sullivan up there on the hard oak chair. That was Patricia's destiny. If she closed this case with a win — and that would be a guilty verdict on two charges of first-degree murder with a double sentence of life in prison without the possibility of parole — she was going to the State Capitol in Lansing, and after that, Washington.

She'd given enough time and money to the leading Democrats of St. Isidore County to know a victory of that magnitude would result in a meteoric rise in her career's trajectory.

Patrica fantasized about this being the last day she'd walk into the St. Isidore County Courthouse while she drove through what passed for morning rush hour traffic in St. Isidore.

The courthouse, next to a ridiculous looking city/county building, where you had to take two different elevators to get to her office, was a testament to the mental midgets who couldn't see any reason to live anywhere else. Built in 1963, with the same kind of cinder blocks that were used to create elementary schools back in the Cold War days, the building usually smelled like her third-grade classroom. Maybe it was the pencil shavings left behind by decades of civil servants. Maybe it was the courthouse cafeteria. But it felt like a school.

However, the building did have the advantage of having lots of windows to let in as much sunshine as possible in a town often covered by clouds bringing rain to St. Isidore if it wasn't snowing or sleeting.

"Since a lot of people are here for a divorce, a trial, or sentencing; the architect figured we needed lots of windows to take advantage of any sunshine possible," Patrica had been told on her first day.

It is such a tiny community pretending to be major, Patricia thought more than once during the past ten years she'd lived in St. Isidore. Home to three minor league teams—hockey, basketball, and baseball—several radio stations staffed by people either on their way up or on their way down the career ladder of broadcasting success; St. Isidore screamed average, as far as Patricia was concerned.

Born and raised in the white-collar suburbs of Detroit, Patricia thought of herself as one of those on her way up and out of Swinging Izzy. She certainly never considered herself to be a lifelong resident of this town. And, it would never be her home.

However, if Judge Leopold sentenced Mary Eileen to anything less than life without parole, or God forbid if the jury came back with a not guilty because of insanity verdict; it would be "Welcome to Walmart" time for Patricia Fry.

Patricia had never taken defeat well. Of course, no one likes to lose. Everyone wants to win. But Patricia was different. She had to win. It's not that her parents drove her unmercifully. It's not that she was sent to bed without dinner for bringing home less than a perfect report card.

It was simply that something inside of Patricia would not allow her to be less than perfect, or even worse, to be defeated.

"Patricia, you have the drive to win, I can't fault you for that," her high school debate coach, Richard Worth told her while they were traveling to the state championship tournament.

Patricia had only nodded. She'd heard about half of what Mr. Worth said. Most of her mind was focused on her team and making sure they didn't stumble. Everything Patricia wanted — doing her undergrad work at Stanford then getting her law degree from Yale or maybe Harvard — was riding on this debate championship.

"But you need to relax," Mr. Worth said. "Winning isn't everything."

God, what tripe, Patricia thought. But she looked at her coach with a very practiced attitude of submission. Of course, you are right; her eyes told adults or anyone who criticized her quest for victory and glory. How foolish of me not to see the truth of what you are saying.

But in her mind, Patricia was screaming, "Why can't these morons just stay out of my way?"

"Patricia, you are not only driven to succeed," a psychiatrist had told her of what was politely called her "nervous breakdown" following a miserable debate team practice.

"You are more than driven, Patricia. You are pathological about winning. You not only ignore the effect you are having on others most of the time; the sliver of time when you do recognize your impact, you simply don't care."

Patricia remembered looking up at Dr. Julianne French with her much-practiced gaze that said, "Gee whiz, how could I have missed that," as the psychiatrist sat on the witness stand. When Patricia started her cross-examination of the good doctor, she could see French had no memory of their time together. As a result, Patricia was driven even more to make the doctor look foolish.

"If you think I was pathological about winning the state high school debate tournament, Dr. French, you should try to read my mind now," Patricia had said to her bathroom mirror while practicing for her day in court.

She was no longer a teenager dreaming of sugar plum fairies with job offers from the largest law firms in America dancing through her head. Patricia Fry focused on Washington. She would pick up Hillary's torch if only she could win this trial.

But, she'd fumbled the opening statement. While Michael Morris was brilliant, eloquent, and dramatic; Patricia had been dreary, drab, and redundant. Her speech had been utterly forgettable. Even Judge Leopold had caught her breath a couple of times and seemed to be pulling for her when Patricia started mumbling words rather than enunciating her thoughts.

"You're trying too hard," Patricia had told herself. "Slow down. Stop if you have too. Give the jury a chance to catch up." However, when she did force herself to stop, Patricia only looked confused.

But she had recovered. Patricia had to admit to herself that she had been nearly magnificent with her witnesses. She had picked Dr. French to pieces. Patricia had attacked the psychiatrist's diagnosis, using the Socratic method of questioning to trap French with her own psychobabble.

The way she laid the case out, there could be no doubt in any juror's mind that Mary Eileen Sullivan knew what she was doing when she'd killed Hans Mueller and David Van Holt. They heard surviving friends and relatives cry on the witness stand. They saw the forensic evidence, the chopped up body parts encased in cement. It was all textbook.

But Patricia also knew that while she had done everything a law professor might want, she'd been talking to herself as much, maybe more, than the jury. She knew she had missed the mark. But fortunately for Patricia, Mary Eileen Sullivan had confessed. She was a killer. And paradoxically, all Patricia had to do was to prove the woman was not crazy.

Her boss, Prosecutor Logan, had slipped her a note reading, "You're batting .500...bottom of the ninth..bases loaded...Knock this bitch out of the park."

Patricia smirked but fought back an urge to look back at Logan. She never liked the military and sports metaphors that her boss threw around to inspire his troops, as Logan put it. There was no need to "knock this bitch out of the park."

Raising an objection to Morris' last question of Mary Eileen had been a mistake. Patricia had been too quick on the trigger and she knew it as soon as the words were out of her mouth. Fortunately, Judge Leopold had overruled her.

Mary Eileen had already dug her own grave. Now, Patricia only had to let Mary Eileen bury herself. She could hardly wait to hear this double-murderer explain to a jury of her peers why killing her ex-husband and then her boyfriend were the acts of a rational woman.

Forty

Staying out of prison wasn't Mary Eileen's prime motivation as she turned the question over in her mind. Were the killings of Hans and David deliberate acts? Were the murders the act of a rational woman? Of course, Mary Eileen wanted to stay out of prison. Her morning sickness that day had been a reminder of her baby, the child that Mary Eileen wanted to raise. Nothing was more important than the love of a mother and daughter. It was a love that Mary Eileen had known as a child. Now it was time to pass that gift on to a child of her own.

Having Sean by her side would have been ideal. But Mary Eileen was raised by a single mother. There was no reason she couldn't do the same thing with her daughter. Mary Eileen wanted Sean. She needed Sean. But Mary Eileen also knew that she rarely got what she wanted. She had always been able to move on. She could do it again.

So, yeah, staying out of prison, having an average life with a child, a dog, a white picket fence and her own business was the goal. But first, Mary Eileen had another task at hand. She had to show these people why they were wrong about her. They needed to understand that she had only done what needed to be done.

"Of course it was rational," Mary Eileen said, dragging out the last word of her declaration. Like a firefly in June; a thought so ugly it was beautiful flickered in her mind just as it did when she began thinking about doing away with David. But this time, she didn't hold on to it. She didn't savor it. Mary Eileen Sullivan left it go.

Rather than launch into a tirade against her attorney, Mary Eileen spoke to the jury, calmly and confidently.

"I said already that David refused to leave, that I wanted to get on with my life," Mary Eileen began. "Of course, there was more. It wasn't just that he was sitting at my dining room table, using my computer, to do his work for the St. Isidore Chronicle." Mary Eileen shot a wicked glance at the press booth. Hastily constructed against the west wall of the courtroom, it held at least ten video cameras from networks around the world, as well as fifty reporters. Even with the journalists packed laptop-to-tablet, Mary Eileen was able to pick out Amanda and Joy. She glared directly into their eyes before she continued.

After shifting her glance to the jury forewoman, Sally Randall, Mary Eileen lowered her voice to a whisper and said, "You know he was a man. And you know that being a man, he was going to get what he thought he deserved." Sally blinked and nodded slightly before Mary Eileen shifted her gaze from one to another of all six women in the jury box.

"What else was I supposed to do?" Mary Eileen said as she turned back to Michael Morris. "He was taking advantage of me. I killed him, yes. Did I want to kill him? No, absolutely not, but David left me no alternative, did he?"

"You didn't have a lawyer to represent you in divorce court?" Morris asked.

"Of course, I did. And look at all the good it did me," Mary Eileen nearly shouted. "You attorneys, up on your podiums, smarter than everyone else, making more money than anyone else, and look what good you do us all."

She swung her gaze back to the jury box, moving her attention from one juror to another, taking her time to make eye contact with the full dozen.

"David was taking advantage of me," Mary Eileen said, concentrating and seemingly enjoying each syllable of the sentence. "My attorney was no help. So the police wouldn't get involved. Therefore I had no other choice. I ended his life because I wanted to be free to live mine."

"And you cut up his body with a chain saw, using cement to hide his arms, legs, torso, and head in your cellar."

Mary Eileen shrugged. "What was done, was done. Again, what choice did I have?"

"You killed Hans Mueller. You shot him with the same gun used to kill David Van Holt, and then you cut up and hid the body parts in your cellar."

"That's right."

"Why? Was he taking advantage of you too?"

Mary Eileen paused, they were beginning to understand, she could feel it.

As she relaxed in the oak chair, she crossed her legs and her arms before saying, "Hans Mueller was even worse. Yes, he was taking advantage of me. He would spend all night with his whores and then come back to my bed."

"His whores?"

"Yes, his whores. Hans Mueller slept with at least ten women in this town, and I can prove it."

"Why didn't you just divorce him?"

"Oh, right," Mary Eileen said. "Look at all the good that did me the last time."

"So, rather than getting a lawyer and filing for divorce, you just killed Hans Mueller. You cut up his body, mixed the cement and carted his body parts down to the cellar under the Coffee Shoppe."

"Again, what choice did I have?" Mary Eileen was sitting up straight now, nearly standing, as Judge Leopold made eye contact with the three court bailiffs to ensure they were ready if the defendant sprang at her attorney.

"He was fucking around on me!"

Judge Leopold slammed the gavel down on her desk. "Mr. Morris, please instruct your client to watch her language. One more outburst like that and I will hold her in contempt of court."

It took Mary Eileen a couple of minutes to bring her breathing back under control.

"He was sleeping around," Mary Eileen said, sneaking a sarcastic look at the judge. "He was sleeping around with every woman who would have him, and bringing those diseases, those STDs, back into my house."

"How could you be sure..."

"I was sure damn, it!" Mary Eileen stood up in the witness booth. Michael Morris recoiled, Patricia jumped to her feet, and the three court bailiffs acted immediately. As they were leading Mary Eileen out of the courtroom, she screamed, "He brought disease into my house. Hans left me no choice. He had to die!"

Patricia trembled as she sat back in her chair. She'd seen drunks lash out in anger in night court, but nothing like Mary Eileen Sullivan's rage. At least a dozen people in the courtroom were standing, reporters pushed and shoved to get by them as they raced for the hallway and the limited bandwidth available for their phones. Video cameramen panted like lustful patrons getting lap dances at the St. Isidore XXX Nightclub. Judge Leopold looked like a blacksmith as she slammed her gavel down, again and again, demanding order in the courtroom.

Patricia looked at Michael Morris, and he at her. As their eyes met, their attention moved to the jury box.

Two of the jurors were crying. Several were standing; others were trembling.

Patricia and Michael didn't speak, but they shared a thought.

Mary Eileen Sullivan had scared the hell out of this jury. She had buried herself.

Forty One

Amanda and Joy decided to eat lunch in shifts after Judge Leopold issued her instructions to the jury and sequestered the twelve St. Isidore citizens who would decide the fate of Mary Eileen Sullivan.

Always the martyr, Joy said, "You eat first. I'll stay here and guard our seats."

Now, she was starving in her martyrdom. But her sacrifice also made sense.

There were easily more than one-hundred reporters in the courtroom listening to Leopold talk to the jury about the difference between finding Mary Eileen guilty of first-degree murder and deciding that she should be considered not guilty because of insanity.

"Remember," Judge Leopold said after she had read the text of the law to the jury, "finding the defendant 'not guilty because of insanity' is not the same as finding her 'innocent.' You can decide that even though Mary Eileen Sullivan has confessed to the murders of David Van Holt and Hans Mueller, and then hiding their bodies, in effect concealing evidence; you can still decide that she was not guilty because she was temporarily insane."

Sally Randall did her best not to wring her hands or show any emotion even though the weight of this civic responsibility rested heavily on her shoulders, while her stomach rumbled, begging for lunch.

The judge's instructions had lasted most of the morning. As Sally and her fellow jury members hung on every word, Judge Leopold also told them that if they came back with a guilty verdict, she would have no choice, under Michigan law, but to sentence Mary Eileen to life in prison with no possibility of parole.

"If they come back with a not guilty verdict, God only knows what my sentence will be," Patricia told Allyson during the long, sleepless night that led to this fateful day.

"If the verdict is 'not guilty by reason of temporary insanity,'" Judge Leopold told the jury, "I will have more discretion in sentencing. My options include sentencing the defendant to a mental health facility of the state's choosing until she is deemed cured, or I could set her free. There is also a full range of possibilities within those parameters."

And if you come back with a simple 'not guilty' verdict, a plethora of opportunities will open for me, Michael Morris thought to himself as he slumped in his wooden chair at the defense table. He was doing his best to look as relaxed as possible. Michael wanted the jury to see that he was supremely certain of victory, even though Mary Eileen seemed anything but confident.

She sat ramrod straight in her chair to the left of Michael, staring straight ahead, her eyes fixed on the clock over Judge Leopold's head. Mary Eileen seemed to be giving the judge her undivided attention. But her mind was far away. It might be Mary Eileen was imagining what life in prison would be like, or perhaps thinking about the possibility of a complete victory, walking away from this courtroom, and back to her life in St. Isidore, or wherever she chose. Mary Eileen knew that if she walked out of the courtroom a free woman, even if she went to a hospital, book and movie deals were waiting.

However, none of that entered her mind.

Instead, she thought only of Sean and their baby.

Mary Eileen was in their backyard, in her mind, playing with their daughter on a swing set, while Sean, wearing cargo shorts, sandals and bare-chested, mowed the lawn. She could see the beads of sweat running down his broad, tanned back as Sean walked away from her and then the smile on his sweaty face as he approached, pushing the power mower.

Their child giggled on the swing, begging her to push her higher and higher, Mary Eileen, barefoot, wearing a light yellow sundress, imagined herself laughing and pretending to push harder and higher.

She looked back over her shoulder, searching for Sean as she heard a loud bang, an explosion perhaps, or maybe a gunshot. Sean was lying face down in the grass. Mary Eileen let go of the swing. She looked down. Their daughter had disappeared.

She heard a second loud bang, followed by a third.

"Jurors, you will now go to the jury room to begin deliberations. The court is recessed until your return," Judge Leopold said as she brought her gavel down the fourth time.

Half an hour later, in the press box, Joy was thinking about her immediate future. Her stomach complained loudly about the lack of food, as she counted down the minutes of Amanda's thirty-minute lunch break. Surely she would be back soon. And she was. Amanda pushed her way through the people standing in the marble-floored hallway and squeezed into the nearly empty courtroom. Ah, Joy thought, finally. But her vision of a Clyde's Diner Big 'C' Burger & Fries in front of her at the restaurant next to the courthouse was dashed when a court bailiff walked to the front of the courtroom and announced, "The jury has reached a verdict."

Mary Eileen, wearing the same gray dress she had worn since the day she first appeared in court, cried, sobbed, and told the judge, "All I can say is that I'm sorry I took the lives of David and Hans."

The jury decision was unanimous.

Mary Eileen had been found guilty of two counts of first-degree murder.

As the jury delivered its verdict, Mary Eileen stood in the same gray dress she had worn during the four-day trial just as stoically as she had listened to the testimony against her.

She didn't blink or flinch when Judge Leopold sentenced her to spend the rest of her life in a women's prison in Jackson, Michigan.

Mary Eileen only nodded to indicate to the judge she understood,

However, she had one more concern, something with which most women who had killed two men didn't have to contend.

Mary Eileen would deal with this, too, she assumed, alone. She was going to have a baby. And perhaps like many women facing prison, she had lost the man she loved, her true love.

As she was walking from the courtroom, Mary Eileen glanced over her shoulder at the audience who had watched her four days of trial and this final day of sentencing.

She looked at the jurors who had decided her fate.

Mary Eileen glanced to the right to look at Judge Leopold one last time.

And she glanced back at the courtroom.

That's when she saw him.

Sean.

He was in the courtroom. He had not deserted Mary Eileen.

Forty Two

The Coffee Shoppe enjoyed near-record business for days following Mary Eileen's sentencing.

This day, Joy and Amanda were in their usual places; sitting on two barstools at the counter facing the front window. They had the best seats in the house to watch traffic move up and down DeVos Avenue while a montage of shoppers, tourists, and business people walked by on the sidewalk, most of whom stopped in for at least a vicarious thrill. It was so much fun to be this close to a killer!

"Did you ever think Christina would take over this place?" Joy said.

"If anyone was going to get it, it had to be her," Amanda said. "She and Mary Eileen were very, very close."

"She's lucky the papers were signed before the police found the bodies downstairs."

"I know," Amanda agreed. "Otherwise the court would have been able to seize the business along with Mary Eileen's apartment."

Mary Eileen had transferred ownership to Christina the day before leaving town in an Uber car. Even before the discovery of the body parts of David and Hans, Mary Eileen was leaving town with no intention of returning to St. Isidore. As far as she was concerned her vacation with Sean was a one-way ticket out of mediocrity.

However, she wanted to be sure the Coffee Shoppe survived and wanted to return the favor of Christina's devotion and loyalty. So Mary Eileen quietly signed the papers to give the business away.

"This is too much," Christina said.

"It is hardly enough for all you have done for me."

"I can't do this. I can't own the Coffee Shoppe."

"If I had ever told myself that I couldn't do it, I never would have started this business," said Mary Eileen. "The only thing standing in your way is your fear. Break through. Be successful. I have no doubt you can do it, and if you let yourself, you will."

"But you are just giving this to me?"

"When Sean and I leave, I don't want ever to have to come back. I don't want anything getting in the way. No attorneys, no closing costs, no terms, no nothing. The business is yours."

"I don't know how..."

Mary Eileen laughed and put both hands on Christina's shoulders. "No one in this town knows better how to run the Coffee Shoppe than you, Christina. No one loves it more than you. You can do this. You have to believe that. I do."

Christina looked down at the ground and then back up at Mary Eileen.

"Maybe I can do this."

"There is no doubt that you will if you let yourself do it. Don't let fear get in the way."

"Thank you."

"No, thank you, Christina. Besides Sean, you are my only friend. And that is the only thing that means more to me than the Coffee Shoppe."

Tears were in Christina's eyes as she signed the papers Mary Eileen handed her. Christina wiped a tear from her cheek as she watched her now former boss walk to the Coffee Shoppe's door for the last time.

Mary Eileen turned the knob on the Coffee Shoppe's glass doors, heard the small bells ring over her head, and took the first steps toward her new life. She was going back to her apartment for one last night.

Mary Eileen spent one more night in her apartment, and she did leave the Coffee Shoppe for good. She just never believed she'd spend the rest of her life behind bars, and the rest of her life without Sean.

During Mary Eileen's trial, there was a sizable contingent in St. Isidore who pitied her and felt her pain. It wasn't sympathy. It was empathy. There were even some on the jury who felt that way, but they all voted to convict her of two counts of first-degree murder. What else was the jury to do? None of the jurors hated Mary Eileen. But she had shocked them. They were scared. Or course, their decision had to be based on the case, the facts of the trial and whether Mary Eileen was guilty of two murders or not guilty because of temporary insanity. But right or wrong, the jurors felt there was a more important question: Did they want to be responsible for letting Mary Eileen Sullivan walk the streets of St. Isidore?

During the press conference that followed the trial, Sally Randall explained to reporters the jury didn't buy the temporary insanity defense. She said that while they considered Mary Eileen's confession and her state of "considerable psychological damage;" there was also the fact that Mary Eileen took lessons in both marksmanship and concrete mixing, along with her decision to flee to Detroit.

As much as she felt Mary Eileen had to go to prison for life when Sally's eyes followed Mary Eileen's, and she saw Sean, Sally was thrilled. It was an emotional moment when his eyes met Mary Eileen's. Sally wasn't the only person on the jury who had been watching Mary Eileen and as a result saw Sean. Joy ran from the courtroom to report the verdict. Amanda stayed behind. So, Sally wasn't the only person with tears in their eyes.

"Sean loved her, still," Amanda said. "No matter what she had done, he loved her."

In fact, Sean had done more than stand by his woman during the most traumatic weeks of her life. Sean conceived and ran the Kickstarter fundraising campaign to pay Micheal Morris more than $750,000.

"I hear Michael Morris is running for Governor in a couple of years," Joy said.

“Could happen. But this I know for sure, Patricia Fry is running for Congress,” said Amanda.

“No way! Who told you that?”

“Ha! You think I’ve forgotten the first thing you taught me?”

“What?”

“Never reveal your sources to the boss.”

“Funny, and true,” Joy said.

“I will say this; there is no doubt the party leadership will endorse her.”

“And after that, who knows where she could go. Nothing will stop her.”

“The only thing she has to fear is her fears,” Amanda said.

She and Joy concentrated on drinking their lattes for the next few minutes, watching a couple of college kids skateboarding down the sidewalk.

“She finally found love. Perhaps it was a little too late, but at least it was love,” Joy said.

“What about Sean? What’s he going to do? The State Police fired him, right?”

“They let him resign. That way he gets to keep his pension, two-thirds of his regular salary.”

“Nice.”

“Yeah, now he can be a stay-at-home dad.”

“A what? You are kidding right?”

“I am serious as a heart attack. Mary Eileen is pregnant. Morris didn’t talk about it at the trial. He wanted to bring it up at sentencing, but she refused.”

“Why?”

“Don’t know. There isn’t any answer for that.”

“But she’s going to keep the baby?”

“Yes, she’ll give birth in prison.”

"Then what?"

"Sean will raise the child, their child. He'll bring the baby to prison whenever he can, as often as he can. Mommy will be in jail for the rest of her life, but she'll get to watch her baby grow up."

"Mary Eileen found true love," said Amanda.

"She just found it too late," said Joy, as she, for the first time, reached for Amanda's hand.

She didn't want to make the same mistake.

Did you love *The Coffee Shoppe Killer*? Then you should read *Janice is Missing: A Crime and Suspense Thriller* by Rod Kackley!

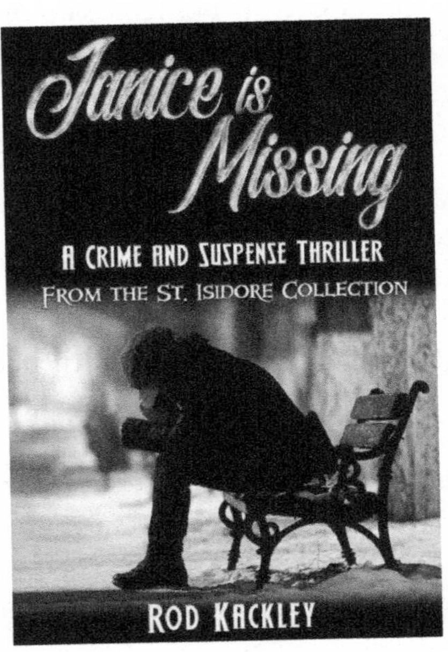

Joy Ellis is a reporter who was looking for a great story. Now she has it. But she also has something more important -- a mission. Joy's decided to do what the entire St. Isidore Police Department has not been able to accomplish -- stop a serial killer.

But what if he stops her first?

Joy has a young reporter on her side, Amanda, and an old, grizzled, cop Jimmy Mack helping her. If they fail, Janice dies. If the worst happens, they're all dead.

Janice is Missing: A Crime and Suspense Thriller is a dark, disturbing crime novel by Rod Kackley that explores the mind of a serial killer hiding in plain sight, the motivations of a young reporter who will do anything for success, and of course, the spirit of Janice.

She's a woman who was ready to take her own life. Now she's fighting to live.

Also by Rod Kackley

Inspired by a Shocking True Crime Story
The Coffee Shoppe Killer

Shocking True Crime Stories
Sleeping With The Devil: A Shocking True Crime Story of the Most Evil Woman in Britain
Who Killed Brittanee Drexel? A Shocking True Crime Story of a Teenager's Murder and a Mother's Grief

St. Isidore Collection
A Wicked Plan: Book 1 From the St. Isidore Collection
Wicked Revenge: Book 2 From the St. Isidore Collection
Wicked Justice: Book 3 From the St. Isidore Collection
Stories of St. Isidore: From The St. Isidore Collection
So Young, So In Love, So Dead: A Serial Killer Thriller
The Suicide Forest

Standalone

Revenge Is Best Served Bloody: A Short Story of WorkPlace Violence, From the St. Isidore Collection
Lies We Tell: A Short Story of Marriage, Infidelity, and Love, From The St. Isidore Collection
Sexual Killing: A Shocking True Crime Story
The Devil Made Him Do It: A Shocking True Crime Story of Mass Murder
Janice is Missing: A Crime and Suspense Thriller
Mommy Deadliest: A Shocking True Crime Story of a Murdering Mother
Sealed With A Kill: A Shocking True Crime Love Story

About the Author

Rod Kackley is an author and journalist living in Grand Rapids, Michigan. He has two adult children a granddaughter on the way (due in October 2015) and a dog, Bella.

Made in the USA
Las Vegas, NV
12 February 2022